FOR THOSE ABOUT TO READ, WE SALUTE YOU!

About the Spartapuss series...

'Cattastic' – London Evening Standard

'Non-stop adventure... Spartapuss serves notice that cattitude rules!' – I Love Cats (USA)

'It's Rome AD36 and the mighty Feline Empire rules the world. This is the diary of slave cat Spartapuss, who finds himself imprisoned and sent off to gladiator school to learn how to fight, for fight he must if he wants to win his freedom. Packed with more catty puns than you ever thought pawsible, this witty Roman romp is history with cattitude.' – Scholastic Junior Magazine

'Spartapuss makes history fun instead of dull...For people who don't like history (like me), this book might change their minds.' – Shruti Patel, aged 10

'I really enjoyed this book and I liked the fact that it was written as if it was Spartapuss's diary. My favourite character was Russell (a crow!!!) Spartapuss's friend. I would recommend this book for ages 10+ especially if you enjoy books with a twist and a sense of humour.'
– Sam (11-year-old Young Archaeologist member from York)

'A truly hilarious story... One of the UK's brightest new authors.' ... 'A must read for children and cat lovers'.
– Teaching and Learning Magazine

'Two paws up! A stylish, witty and thoroughly engaging tale that will captivate young and old readers alike.'
– Tanuja Desai Hidier, author of 'Born Confused'
(Winner of the London Writer's Award for Fiction 2001)

'...a unique couple of books that have really caught the imagination of the public here... clearly something special.' – Andrew Fairmaner (buyer, The British Museum)

'This fantastic tale of the Roman Empire ruled by cats is a must for children and adults alike... This is a really fantastic tale! With another three in the series, there's more adventure to come.' – Sarah, Ottakar's East Grinstead

'Catligula's reign, a time when cats ruled Rome, was short if bloody, a story told by freedcat Spartapuss, employed as a scribe by Catligula, whose life was saved by Spartapuss. The Emperor is mad, poisoning those he believes to be his enemies and making his pet, Rattus Rattus, a member of the Senate. The Spraetorian Guard are determined to end his reign before Catligula ruins the empire.

Based loosely upon the writings of classical historians, Catligula is the second in a series that re-tells the scandals of the early Caesars in an accessible form, inevitably reminiscent of Robert Graves' *I, Claudius*. The jokes lie mainly in the names – the Greeks become Squeaks – but the descriptions of life in classical Rome are good, particularly the set piece in the Arena, when Catligula plays himself in what must have been an embarrassing display to even his sycophantic feline audience.

Readers who know the original stories will enjoy the fun, and those who don't know the history may be enticed to look more closely at the Roman stories.'
– The School Librarian, Vol 53 no 4, 2005

'This is too good to be left just as a children's book! Extremely funny and brilliantly written. Robin Price has taken the events of Roman history focusing around the time of Emperors Tiberious, Caligula and Claudius and turned it into something fascinating.'
– Monsters and Critics.com

DIE CLAWDIUS

ROBIN PRICE

MOGZILLA

DIE CLAWDIUS

First published by Mogzilla in 2006

Paperback edition:
ISBN 10: 0-9546576-8-3
ISBN 13: 978-0-9546576-8-0
Hardback edition:
ISBN 10: 0-9546576-7-5
ISBN 13: 978-0-9546576-7-3

www.mogzilla.co.uk

Printed in Great Britain by Mackays of Chatham, Chatham, Kent

The author would like to thank the following
people (and their friends) for all of their help and encourage-
ment:
Michele, Peter, Hayley, Christina G, Sam, Phil, Annabel, Rupert,
Nick, Ricky, John G, Sinc, Andrew, Bev, Les, Kirsty, Claire
E, Twiz, Ed, Arvind, Tanuja, Bernard, Jon, Olivia, Am, Ben,
David, Mum and Dad, Nicole, Catherine B, Nicholas R, Guy G,
Caroline C and Rupert.

For Scarlet...

THE TALE SO FAR...

DIE CLAWDIUS is the third book in the SPARTAPUSS series. It is set in Roman times in a world ruled entirely by cats, where humans have never existed.

In I AM SPARTAPUSS, the first book in the series, SPARTAPUSS is comfortable managing Spatopia, Rome's finest Bath and Spa. He is a loyal servant to his master CLAWDIUS – a cat of the Imperial Family.

But Fortune has other plans for him. There is a nasty incident in the vomitorium. It causes offence to 'CATLIGULA' the would-be heir to the cushioned throne. SPARTAPUSS is thrown into prison, only to be released into Gladiator training school. At the end of his training, he is given a golden coin by his mentor TEFNUT. He fights at the Games and is freed by CATLIGULA. This causes CLAWDIUS much annoyance, for he has now lost a valuable slave. Shortly afterwards, SPARTAPUSS rescues CATLIGULA from the wreckage of a chariot crash.

CATLIGULA is the second book in the series. When CATLIGULA becomes Emperor, his madness brings Rome to within a whisker of disaster. He poisons those he believes are his enemies and makes his pet RATTUS RATTUS a senator. The SPRAETORIAN

GUARD plot to get rid of him and need SPARTAPUSS to help. SPARTAPUSS agrees but at the last minute changes his mind and helps CATLIGULA to escape. He convinces the Emperor that he is needed to perform a play. During the performance, the Arena is flooded in mysterious circumstances and CATLIGULA is lost. The Emperor's PURRMANIAN BODYGUARDS go on the rampage, looking for revenge for the death of their master. They find CLAWDIUS (CATLIGULA's uncle) hiding on top of a cupboard. On SPARTPUSS'S suggestion, they pronounce that CLAWDIUS is Emperor of the Known World.

In DIE CLAWDIUS, the third book in the series, SPARTAPUSS is summoned to the Palace by NARKITTUS, one of the Emperor's new advisors.

DRAMATIS PAWSONAE

Who's who!

From the deserts of Fleagypt to the forests of Purrmania, The Feline Empire rules most of the known world. The Land of the Kitons (known as 'the wet island') has not been thought worth conquering.

The Romans:

Clawdius – Emperor of Rome

Narkittus – The Emperor's advisor

General Mawlus – Rome's grumpiest general

Vespurrsian – a promising young Army commander

The Kitons:

Todimpuss (TDP) – a Prince of the Kitons

Caractapuss (Carac) – his brother (also a Prince)

Furg – a young Mewid (of the Micini tribe)

Others:

Captain Kat – a sea captain

Old Kat – his father

Tefnut – a mystic

Find out more at www.mogzilla.co.uk

MAIUS XXVI

May 26th

Ship's log

THIS IS THE CHRONICLE of Spartapuss, most miserable of cats. I am on board The Stroker, most miserable of ships, headed for the land of my birth. I am told that it is a perfect place to be miserable in, for it is the land closest to the Land of the Dead. How I am sick of the sea. And I am sick of the wailing of the seagulls. Blow wind, and crack their beaks! Blow us onwards, to the land of my miserable ancestors.

MAIUS XXVII

May 27th

There is no wind. The ship drifts on a sea as flat as a rabbit pancake. The sailors are growling that we could be stuck here for days. Old Kat has them constantly busy cleaning the ship and mending ropes – otherwise they would have their thieving paws all over our luggage by now, no doubt. As there is nothing else to do I shall record the cruel events that brought me to this place. I shall no longer ask the Goddess Fortune for help, as she has abandoned me.

THE LETTER

To help the hours to pass faster on this lonely ship, I will tell how I came to this place. All wars, great or small, have to start somewhere. The ones that I have read about usually start with a small detail, the sort of thing that old professors like to use to amuse their students with. This war began with a letter.

> *To the idiot Clawdius,*
>
> *Give us back the WOMPS that the traitor Vericat stole from us. Do as I command or things will go very badly for you.*
>
> *Yours with spite,*
>
> *Todimpuss, King of all the Kitons.*

"Womps?" asked the Emperor Clawdius, with a half hiss.

"Weapons, Caesar," began Narkittus, who was usually ready with an answer before his Emperor had finished the question.

"W.O.M.P. stands for Weapon of Magical Power, Caesar," explained General Mawlus.

Narkittus may be the Emperor's most trusted adviser (which isn't saying much) but he was an ex-slave and not even a Roman. The General wasn't going to listen to another of his lectures.

"Weapons of Mewidic power," corrected Narkittus.

The General let out a hiss. He had come straight from the Senate where Rome's most important citizens were already gossiping about the rude letter from the terrible Kiton King. The letter was supposed to be top secret, but tongues at the Palace grow looser with each day of Clawdius's rule. "The Senate is agreed Caesar," said Mawlus, ignoring Narkittus. "The Kitons must pay dearly for this insult. I have three legions ready for an invasion, but if a fourth could be spared, it would speed our victory."

Clawdius's thin whiskers twitched as he read the letter again. A slave came forward with a bowl of his favourite chicken with oyster and wild mushroom sauce and he passed it to the Imperial Taster to check for poison. I thought at that time what a marvellous job the tasters have. They get to sample every scrap of food or drop of drink that passes the Emperor's lips - Rome has never known an Emperor that ate badly. I even applied for such a job myself once but the head cook said I do not have the right nose for it. During the test I passed a bowl of baked cod as fit to eat, mistaking the smell of a deadly poison for a touch too much black pepper in the oyster sauce.

General Mawlus couldn't stand it any longer. He began to flick his tail in open impatience.

"What shall we tell the Senate, Caesar?"

Clawdius studied the letter and without looking up asked:

"What would you have me do Narkittus? The Kitons are a lot of hot heads. These Womps are obviously very important to them. Have you thought about giving them back?"

"Giving them back?" spat the General, bristling.

I must confess that I have never liked Narkittus. He is always sniffing around the Emperor looking for a way to make himself more powerful. It is said that he has more influence over Clawdius than any wife! But this idea was daring even by his standards.

"Rome has never been poorer. Catligula spent a fortune, four fortunes in fact, before you became Emperor," said Narkittus. "We cannot afford a costly foreign war unless there is treasure, but the only thing in that miserable land you are sure to return with is a cold."

Before General Mawlus could answer, there was a terrible scream. The taster fell upon his face and clutched his stomach. Something was wrong with the chicken.

"D-d-d-doctor!" spluttered the Emperor.

The rest of the room took up the shout. Where were the doctors when you needed them? There was a General wailing and scratching of claws upon the floor tiles.

"Is Caesar ill? Did he touch the meat?" said General Mawlus, without panic.

"Not for me – for the t-taster" said Clawdius.

"Trust us Caesar, we will do everything in our power to save his life," said a doctor who had just arrived.

"N-Never mind his life. Find out about the poison. Who did this? I must know," said Clawdius.

Long months of training meant that he had almost cured his stutter, except in times of extreme excitement like this.

"What about the Kitons, Caesar?" asked Mawlus.

"Write back to the Kitons. Remind them that I am the Roman Emperor. And say I am n-not used to being insulted like that."

And so it seemed that Fortune smiled upon the Kitons, for Clawdius had given them a second chance. We heard no more of the matter for two months. Then the Emperor received a second letter.

To the idiot Clawdius,

You are a liar, as well as a fool. You are used to being insulted. It is said that your own family call you a half-wit and a weakling.

Give us back our Womps, or you will DIE C-C-CLAWDIUS.

Yours with more spite,

Todimpuss, King of all the Kitons

And with that the matter was as good as settled. The invasion of the Land of the Kitons was the talk of the city. Which Generals would the Emperor send? There were triumphs to be won. Official triumphs are only awarded to Generals lucky enough to prove how brave they were by leading their armies into battle on foreign soil. You get to dress up in a purple collar and parade around the Arena in a chariot with everyone cheering and throwing fish at you. There is no greater honour in public life, as everyone knows.

THE CALL UP

The next day I was surprised to find myself summoned to the Palace. I arrived late at the doors of the Emperor's private apartments, bristling after an argument with the Spraetorians at the gate. They did not recognise me. It is many weeks since I have been called to the Palace, although I still draw my scribe's salary. The reason is that Narkittus, the Emperor's adviser, has introduced his own scribes who can write good letters in both Catin and his native Squeak. It seems that I am no longer needed. I was stung by this silence, for I knew our Emperor when he was plain Clawdius, owner of a bathhouse. I saved his life once so he sometimes used to look to me for advice. Well not 'look to me' exactly but I used to give him advice whether he asked for it or not. But now it seems that I am not needed. For Narkittus has go his claws in everything at the

Palace. It is said that he has Clawdius on a short lead and haunts his every step.

I padded into the room to find Clawdius sitting on his cushioned throne and next to him were General Mawlus and Vespurrsian – one of the General's more promising young officers. Narkittus was there (of course) with his many servants waiting on his every word. Clawdius was in a state of nervous excitement and struggled to get his words out properly. They had been discussing Womps. It was the first time I had heard the word and I confess that at the time I had no clue what they were talking about. Clawdius's grey eyes flickered and his tail began to twitch in annoyance.

"Magical weapons? No one in their right mind believes in that!" laughed Vespurrsian.

Clawdius said nothing. Vespurrsian did not know Clawdius as I did. Our Emperor was most superstitious and clearly believed in magical weapons.

"We will do as you command Caesar," said General Mawlus, softening his voice, "but please take the advice of an old soldier. Your place is here, in Rome."

"I am g-going," said Clawdius.

"But the Land of the Kitons is a land full of dangers," growled the General.

"That's why I'm sending Narkittus along first, to make arrangements for my arrival," said Clawdius.

"You want to to take this Squeak freedcat?" hissed General Mawlus, bristling. "That will not be necessary, Caesar. Soldiering usually is best left to the Generals."

"Who usually leave it to the soldiers," said Narkittus under his breath.

"Here is a letter. It is signed by a hundred of our most experienced Senators, all begging you to stay in Rome," said Mawlus, trying a final appeal.

"That settles it. I'm c-c-coming," said Clawdius. "My wife is right. Leading the invasion is the only way to get my enemies in the Senate to take me seriously."

Narkittus looked pleased at this. For a moment I wondered if he and Clawdius's wife had come up with the whole idea together. There have been three plots to kill him already, and it is said that she is behind two of them for sure.

"Great Caesar..." began Mawlus.

"Enough!" said Clawdius. "Narkittus will go with you and prepare for my arrival. I can't have General Mawlus - my military genius, c-c-conquering the best bits of the land and grabbing all the glory before I arrive, c-can I?"

Clawdius often spoke the truth, as if it was a joke. It was a habit he had learned from Catligula.

"Officers, you have your orders," said Narkittus with a smile.

Clawdius waved them off. I was padding towards the door, thinking about dinner when Narkittus said:

"Not you Spartapuss. You can stay."

I do not know how, but Narkittus had persuaded the Emperor that I must accompany him to the Land of the Kitons. Worse still, I was to go in the very first ship of the invasion fleet. Suspecting that this was Narkittus's plan to get rid of me, I knew that I must beg the Emperor to change his mind. Although my life depended on it, my tongue was tied in knots.

"It is a dark land, full of dangerous barbarians," I protested.

"Yes," said Clawdius.

"It is said that they have magic weapons," I gasped, "and no underfloor heating," I added.

"It is worse than that," said Narkittus. "The Land of the Kitons is a backward land full of wild tribes who hate each other even more than they hate Rome. It is ruled by savage kings who spit hatred and wage bloody wars over small matters like garden fences and fishing rights. It is a roadless, charmless, hopeless wasteland, with tasteless food."

Now I have no great love for the Land of the Kitons – although I was born there. I have never set paw in that unhappy place since I was a kitten. But to hear Narkittus listing so many bad things about it made me bristle. I tried to think of some clever reply, but all I could say was:

"I hear that the food is not so bad when you get used to it."

"You'll have plenty of time to get used to it," said Narkittus.

"But Emperor, please!" I begged, turning to Clawdius,

"It is as I said, Caesar. Didn't I tell you that he would resist?" crowed Narkittus.

Clawdius rang the bell on his collar and at once his Purrmanian bodyguards arrived. They were accompanied by two wiry looking characters, both strangers to the bathhouse by the smell of them.

"Take him away!" ordered Narkittus.

"Shall we give him a taste of the whip, Caesar?" asked the first.

The guards could not believe it. In the Emperor Tiberius's day it was death to speak to the Emperor without getting permission first. Things under Clawdius were really going to the dogs. Even Catligula, who went mad, liked the old traditions and kept up discipline by flogging his slaves once a month whether they deserved it or not.

"If he resists – uphold the law," ordered Narkittus.

The last thing I remember before being bundled into a basket was the look of extreme satisfaction on Narkittus's face. I decided then to buy a curse for him as soon as we reached the Land of the Kitons. Narkittus is jealous and cannot stand it when others have the Emperor's ear. Because I served Clawdius in the old days, he has taken a dislike to me. Am I to be done away with?

PORT AND CUPBOARD

So it was that I awoke with a thumping headache, in a wooden cupboard. I'd been kidnapped and dragged off by a gang of foul smelling sailors, with no chance to say goodbye to my friends! How I wished that my old teacher Tefnut was there to help me. But there had been no sniff of her for months. That's the problem with mystics – you can never get hold of them when you need them.

I later learned that the cupboard was in fact one of the larger cabins on board the ship. And it was a better cabin than I deserved according to the Captain's mate, a gruff fellow with no whiskers, torn ears and a face more scar than fur. He crashed through my door and bellowed that the Captain wanted to see me that evening. But in the meantime, I was ordered to stay below decks. He said he'd have to chain me up in irons if I disobeyed. He did not mention dinner, except to offer to give me a taste of something called 'the dog of nine tails' if I misbehaved. It is said that 'rations' on board ships are basic, and there are a lot of hard biscuits involved, but serving dog to the passengers is going a bit far.

That evening I met Captain Kat, who was less grumpy than the miserable mate. He explained that I was not a prisoner, but while I was on board his ship, I was his responsibility. He said it would be better for all of us if I stayed 'below' for now. Being kept below deck is perhaps the worst part of life at sea. There is none of the adventure, but all of the discomfort. As I sat in this creaky old ship, with the constant rocking of the waves, my thoughts began to run. I wondered what Narkittus had said to Clawdius to make him decide to lead his armies into battle. Was Narkittus in the pay of Clawdius's wife? Clawdius is no fighter. When he was young, his illness stopped him from joining in military training. I wondered about the Womps. At first Narkittus said we should give the Kitons their magic weapons back. Now he wanted Clawdius to bring them along – to taunt the Kitons before the battles. I decided that Narkittus is a weather vane – his arguments change as the wind of opinion blows this way and that.

STEP ASIDE BELOW

Two days and nights passed and I thought of our ship on the long voyage to Maul and then on to the Land of the Kitons. And every day was a day further away from dear Rome. The air had a stale taste below decks and I longed for a sight of the sun. The constant rocking of the ship made me feel sick sometimes but I was a little pleased with myself for getting used to ocean life so quickly. The Kitons are said to be a seafaring lot so perhaps I have some sea salt in my blood?

I remembered Captain Kat's orders to stay below deck. But orders are there to be disobeyed so I decided to risk a sniff around. It didn't take long before I found a suitable hatch. I padded carefully up the narrow stairs, pressed my nose against the hatch and it opened. Out on deck the fresh air tasted fine. I ran to the side of the ship that the sailors call 'port', and was amazed at what I saw. We were still in port, being loaded!

The deck was as busy as a beehive. Actually, it was more of a wasps' nest, with angry sailors cursing at each other and hissing at the loaders to pull harder as they hauled the heavy ropes to get the cargo on board. For Romans do not pack light when they go on an invasion.

At the centre of this whirlpool was Captain Kat – barking out orders in some strange language that only sailors seem to know – avast this, belay that, trim the sail, splice the braces, and so on.

I have no clue how the crew could hear these instructions as they were so busy cursing the loaders and each other. I heard a voice close by me shouting:

"ASIDE BELOW!"

I was trying to work out what this could mean when another shout came:

"STEP ASIDE BELOW!"

Then something got a hold of my collar and tugged hard.

"NEPTUNA'S NAILS! STEP ASIDE YOU BAG OF DIRT!" spat a sailor, giving me a sour look.

A heavy crate fell like a stone and crashed into the

space where I'd just been sitting.

It was a whisker-close call. I was thinking that a good deal of the words in the sailor's language must be curses, when I noticed the writing on the crate in front of my nose:

DO NOT OPEN ON PAIN OF DEATH

NARKITTUS

Below Narkittus's name I saw the Imperial seal. I got my breath back and struggled to the side of the ship. Perhaps Narkittus really was trying to kill me! There was something unusual about that crate that set me thinking, apart from the ON PAIN OF DEATH warning, which is written on most imperial goods. The loaders take no notice of such warnings – it would be about as much use to write FRAGILE – DO NOT DROP on it. At any rate, there was something out of the ordinary about this crate. It was too faint to smell, it was more of a feeling. I decided that I had tasted enough fresh air, so I crept back below deck. But dare I wait till nightfall to try to escape?

STOP WATCH

As soon as darkness fell I decided to leave. I retraced my steps, but when I pushed my nose against the hatch it would not move. It must have been blocked by cargo. I began to curse at myself like a sailor. What if I was trapped now and the ship sailed before I could get off? Why hadn't I taken my chance to escape? Then I spotted a point of light and padded silently towards the other end of the corridor. Moonlight poured through the gaps in the deck above me. Then I saw it - a hatch just like the other. This one was easy to shift and in a moment I was out on deck, watching the city lights dance. I knew that my best chance to get away was a thick cable that ran from the prow of the ship down to the dockside. I am no great climber but soon I was halfway down that rope – trying to calm my pounding heart and will myself not to look down at the black water below me. I inched my way down the cable and was almost clear when I heard a shout below:

"Stop! Stay still in the name of the Emperor!"

It was the Watch. I might have guessed that the team of watchers would be doubled for the loading of The Dogless. For the first ship in the Emperor's invasion fleet was an important departure. Unfortunately the Watch had actually been watching for a change, rather than playing dice all night as is usual.

As I ran down the cable, which suddenly seemed thinner now, I could think of nothing but dry land. I could hear the Watch behind me as a stepped onto the dock and bolted for cover. Any hiding place would do. Thanking Peus that I had lost them, I crept behind a pile of empty packing crates and slipped inside the first one I could find. As soon as I got the lid closed, I knew that the crate wasn't empty. A voice said:

"Make no sound, or the Watch will hear us."

"Tefnut? I whispered, recognising the voice of my old friend and teacher. "What in Peus' name are you doing here?"

"Hiding," she replied.

"Fortune be praised!" I gasped. "You've come to help me escape."

"No," she replied, "I am come to help you back on board the ship."

"But they're invading the Land of the Kitons!" I said. "I don't want to go."

"Really?" she asked, as if surprised that I did not want to be a part of Clawdius's war.

"Yes, really," I replied with a hiss.

Tefnut sniffed and did not reply. She gave one of her long pauses. I knew that she had more to say.

Finally, it came. "Listen to your heart," she said. "Haven't you always dreamed that you would return before the end?"

Never pick an argument with a mystic, for you seldom get the last word. Annoyingly, she was right. In secret, I had often wondered what it would be like to see the land where I was born and perhaps find my tribe – maybe even some relations. I have always felt as if only half of me belonged in Rome. The other half would always be a stranger here. I once confessed this to Russell, but he didn't understand.

"Everyone feels like that when the wind comes from the east," he told me.

"I thought I might go to the Land of the Kitons one day for a visit, not for an invasion," I hissed. "Besides, Narkittus is trying to kill me."

Tefnut sighed. "If Narkittus wanted you dead… ," she began.

The thud of an upturned crate cut her off in mid sentence. We heard scratches and shouts. The Watch were beginning to search the row of crates where we were hiding.

Like oil from a bottle, Tefnut poured through a hole in the side of our crate. I am not built for tight squeezes and by the time I'd hauled myself out there was no sign of her. The whiskers on my right side gave a twitch. At first I thought it was the salt air, but sure enough I noticed a shape in the shadows creeping out towards the dockside. She stopped for a moment, her huge eyes shining against the moon. She looked back, encouraging me to follow – as a mother bird wills the last of her babies to fly the nest. I was all set to follow her when I saw her intention. She sprung onto the end of the cable and began to climb up towards the ship.

But alas, I did not follow my mystic friend. For nothing, not even Paws himself, could convince me to get back onto that rotten ship. I gave out a hiss to that effect and the Watch heard us.

I am ashamed to say that there was nothing I could do to help. The Watch had now got scent and sight of her and I knew by her look that my help would be no help at all. Her easiest means of escape was up the

31

cable, onto the moored ship. But alas poor Tefnut had other plans. Her purpose was to get me back on board the ship – she didn't want the guards following her.

It was thirty tails or more from her position half-way up the cable to the dockside below. She turned back on herself and hurtled down the cable towards the stunned guards. At the last moment she sprung out towards the dockside. I heard no splash but the Watch were soon gathered around the dockside shining lights. Some time must have passed, for the sky was brown like the hour before dawn. Their lights had stopped bobbing. As far as I could tell they discovered nothing.

When I was sure that no one could see me, I crept into the first hiding place I could find, a crate full of dried meat. I was in no mood for food but there was nowhere else to hide. I dared not move for fear of the guards discovering me. I must have fallen fast asleep for I woke with a jolt. I listened carefully, hoping for the familiar jolt of cartwheels on ruts. After endless scuffling and banging, my crate finally came to rest. I knew what had happened before I had the lid of my hiding place open. The familiar rocking gave it away. My crate had been carried aboard the ship.

MAIUS XIV

May 14th

Back on Board

Now that we are under way, I am sick. Not just seasick, but sick in my heart. I have no clue what has happened to poor Tefnut. The sailors say the Watch found nothing so she is either escaped or drowned. Either way she is free. Her wish has been granted as I am back on board. Now we are out of sight of the land, no one can follow us. The wind fills our sails and blows me far from my dear city, which I know I will never see again.

MAIUS XV

May 15th

Captain Kat came to visit me today in my cabin. I was expecting to be thrown into whatever passes for a prison here for leaving his ship without permission. I am sure he must have noticed that I was missing from my cabin so I decided to apologise for 'getting lost'. He told me not to trouble myself. The matter was settled. Now we are on the open sea, I am allowed to roam above decks, and go wherever I like.

I was so pleased not to be punished that I congratulated him on being the Captain of one of Caesar's finest warships. He gave me a strange look – as if he'd found a rotten prawn in his fish pie.

I later learned that this is not a ship of war. It is merely a hired luggage ship transporting the baggage that is needed for the invasion. The soldiers have gone in their own warships, which are faster than ours. That is why we are the first ship to depart. News of great importance is that I am not the only passenger on board. There is another who has been asking after me, so the Captain has invited us both to dinner tomorrow when I will be introduced. I cannot wait. The sailors are poor company – constantly asking me if I would like to bet money on silly things like which grain sack a rat will leap onto next. I am certain they have the rats trained, for I lost a day's biscuits yesterday. I am looking forward to some civilised conversation.

MAIUS XVII

May 17th

THE CAPTAIN'S dinner was a great disappointment. "Spartapuss – I'll leave you to introduce yourself to our guest," said Captain Kat. "I have duties to do, so I will not be joining you for dinner."

"We've already met," I said. "But please excuse

me. I'm feeling rather sick. The sea has been getting rougher and rougher since this afternoon."

"You call this rough?" laughed the Captain. "She's as still as a puddle in summer."

"Please Captain, may I be excused?" I groaned. "My poor stomach couldn't stand a sea biscuit."

"Do as you wish," said Captain Kat.

As I left the Captain's cabin, my heart was in my mouth. My fellow passenger was none other than Narkittus. Of course I dared not eat with him, for he has a reputation as a poisoner. I heard from one of the crew that he was due to travel with General Mawlus but the General would not stand to have a Squeak freedcat on his flagship. Mawlus left him sitting on the dockside and sailed off. The mate, who was passing when I heard this, went on to say that he thinks that Squeaks like Narkittus are worse even than the Kitons, who are at least pure savages and do not pretend to be civilised. His view on freedcats is no better: "Once a slave, always a slave," is his motto. I said nothing when I heard this, for I too am a slave who has won his freedom. But I held my tongue - it is a two thousand mile swim to the Land of the Kitons, in some of the coldest seas in this world or the next!

MAIUS XVIII

May 18th

A Light in the Skies

THERE WAS A great light in the skies today, which the sailors took as a good omen from Neptuna, the Lord of the Water. They are the most superstitious group that I have ever known. And at last they've had a sign worth interpreting. The light shot like an arrow in the direction of the Land of the Kitons. Narkittus noted it too, as he was on deck for some sky gazing. The sailors say that because of the sign we are sure to have good wind tomorrow. Most of them have it already, on account of their diet of hard ships' biscuit.

MAIUS XIX

May 19th

TODAY THE WIND picked up and we made good progress. The sailors were not at all surprised, putting it down to the light we saw in the skies yesterday. Also, we are being followed by a school of mackerel, which is said to be another good omen. For an oily fish will never follow a ship into danger, or so it is said!

MAIUS XX

May 20th

I WAS SADDENED today to see that our friends the mackerel have disappeared. I sat all day and watched for them but there was no sign. However we seem to have picked up some new friends. I caught a glimpse of a couple of dolphins playing in the waves at sundown – a pretty sight. Oh the joy of life on the ocean waves!

MAIUS XXI

May 21st

T HOSE ARE NOT dolphins! They are tiger sharks – the scourge of the deep. According to the crew, they are the most dangerous type of shark known. For once they catch sight of you on deck they will follow your ship for weeks and stalk you like lions.

"Perhaps they ought to be called lion sharks," I said, rather pleased with myself.

The crew did not laugh at my joke, as they were too busy running away from the rail to stay out of sight of the sharks.

MAIUS XXIV

May 24th

Shark Watch

THE SHARKS HAVE been following us for three days now and the sailors are begging me to stay below deck. The sharks appear whenever I am in sight, it is said.

Narkittus looks worried. Perhaps the sharks have spotted him as well. This morning he began to prepare offerings to Mewpiter, and Purrcury, who is the messenger of the Gods, but also deals with travellers, actors and thieves. When our Captain saw the smoke from Narkittus's burning incense he became furious and demanded that our Squeak friend put his fire out.

"I will not," said Narkittus in a superior voice – as if he was telling off a new servant at the Palace.

The Captain did not answer but grabbed hold of a broom and swept the offerings overboard, fire and all. The crew, who had gathered around to watch, gave a great cheer.

"Have you forgotten who I am?" hissed Narkittus, ignoring their shouts.

"Have you forgotten where you are?" growled the Captain. "Never sacrifice to the land gods on a ship. The sea gods are quick to anger." Dropping his voice he continued in a low whisper. "All the crew are superstitious, they already think that you have brought trouble aboard. They respect the Lord of the Water – if you ignore their wishes, on your own head be it." Then the Captain ordered the restless crew back to their work.

MAIUS XXV

May 25th

Pirate Rock

WE HAVE NOT reached the Land of the Kitons yet and already I have seen enough adventure to fill a whole ship's journal. What I must now record will turn the blood as cold as sea water.

A moment after our Captain put Narkittus's fire out it began to pour with rain. The sharks, who had been dogging us, dropped below the surface. I was pleased to be rid of them. But soon a terrible wind got up. "Claws out lads," said Captain Kat. "It's too late to trim the sail. We'll have to ride this one out."

With our sail still up we drove on through waves as big as villas, praying that the storm would blow itself out.

Two hours later there was no sign of the wind dropping and the crew were beginning to tire. Twice the waves broke over the wooden rail at the prow of the ship and I clung on by my claws. It was all I could do to stop myself from being washed away. The day grew darker and the wind screamed across the deck. All the clouds had come together to form a single great brute of a cloud, which grew blacker by the minute.

"Look out!" cried the lookout.

I remember being pleased to hear someone doing their job properly.

"Rocks ahead!" cried the mate.

The fog lifted for a moment to reveal a great black rock – jagged, like a bad tooth just pulled.

The crew cried out in panic and rushed to the oars, for we thought we might row our way free. At last there was a slight dip in the wind, just enough for us to get the sail down. All on board took an oar, save the Captain and Narkittus. We rowed for our very lives, but every oar stroke away from that black rock was in vain, for the current drew us two strokes towards it. Soon the crew began to tire and cry out to the Gods to save them.

"Courage lads," cried the Captain. "Take it in turns to row so you do not tire yourselves. We must lighten our load. Throw anything overboard that is not nailed down."

In order to save the ship the crew began to throw the cargo overboard. Soon barrels and crates were bobbing about in our wake.

"It's all or nothing lads," said the Captain. "We must be lighter or we'll surely be broken up."

Then the crew began to wail and started to tear the

ship to pieces. Decking, rope and spare sails, even the nails themselves were thrown over the side.

Then the mate, who had been silent throughout all this, threw down his oar and said:

"It ain't no good Captain. We'll tear the ship in two, but we'll never get away. We must pay the ferry-man."

There were shouts of agreement.

It was unfortunate that Narkittus chose that very moment to show his face on deck as the sailors had decided that a sacrifice was needed, whether to their Gods or to the rock, I have no clue.

Three sailors had a hold of his precious crate and were trying to heave it over the side, but it was too heavy to shift.

"Tell these dogs to get their paws off my luggage Captain," he snapped, "or in Caesar's name I will flog them myself."

"Put down his luggage lads," laughed the mate. "I think it's time we paid our fare."

And with that he seized Narkittus and dragged him over to the side of the ship.

Narkittus twisted free and leapt up on top of his precious crate. He was surprisingly calm now as he tried to reason with the mob.

"What in Peus's name do you think you will achieve by sacrificing me to a rock? In Rome we honour the proper Gods, not things of nature, like lakes and rivers. You might as well worship sticks and stones."

Before these words had left his mouth there was a mighty crack and a bolt of lightning hit the mast and snapped it clean in two. The top part of it crashed over the side, taking the sail with it.

The crew rolled on their bellies on the deck and covered their eyes.

"He's right!" hissed Captain Kat. "Get up shipmates. Unless it's mutiny you're thinking of."

But as the crew got to their feet, the mate let out a dreadful wail. "It's got eyes!" he cried.

Turning to that terrible rock I saw two fiery eyes through the mist, flickering as if there was some cold intelligence behind them. This was too much for the crew.

"Over the side with him! Send him to Neptuna or you'll never see your homes again," hissed the mate, in a panic.

I must confess that I didn't feel that sorry for Narkittus. He was an arrogant bully and was about to get his reward for a lifetime of rudeness. The Captain and I looked at each other.

"It's mutiny. If we let them throw him over, it'll be us next," growled Captain Kat.

"For what it's worth, I am with you Captain," I said drawing myself up to my full height.

Just then a shout went up from the lookout. "Ship ahoy! Ship ahoy!"

In their delight, the crew forgot Narkittus for a moment.

"A rescue ship! Thank Peus, we are saved!" I shouted, jumping up into the rigging to get a better look. I saw that my friends the sharks were back.

"Get down before they skin us all alive! That's a pirate ship," growled the Captain.

We waited, helpless, as the strange ship drew nearer. With our mast taken out by the lightning strike there was no escape.

"Is there no hope?" I asked.

The Captain said nothing and pointed to the portside rail where a mass of rats were gathering. They were fleeing their nests and throwing themselves overboard to swim towards the pirate ship, which was now alongside us.

"Cowards! Where are you going?" shouted the Captain.

"Stop 'em lads! When the rats leave the ship, the game is up," he growled.

"Why don't we just pay the pirates to take us out of here?" I asked.

"We'll pay all right," moaned the mate. "They're bloodthirsty cut-throats. You can't just hire them out like a pleasure boat."

Suddenly, a heavy object bounced off the rail and clattered onto the deck. It was a bucket, tied to a long rope. Inside it was a note:

Your ship has been taken by THE PIRATE KING. Put your gold and valuables into this bucket. Note to Captains, heroes etc. Do not resist! Throw yourself overboard now and save yourselves the trouble of a bitter end, for we are a heartless crew of CUT-THROATS.

When he read this note Captain Kat began to dance about the deck. I have heard it said that the brave 'dance at danger' but I didn't think I'd ever be near enough to see it happen. Then Captain Kat leapt onto the rail and shouted: "Ahoy! The Stroker?"

So it turned out that by a lucky spin of Fortune's Wheel we had crossed claws with Captain Kat's father, Old Kat who is also a Captain. Old Kat was out doing a bit of wrecking on the black rock. The 'eyes' we'd seen on the rock were fires, lit to lure unsuspecting ships into his trap. For once ships were held by the strong current, their crews would soon exhaust themselves by rowing and were easy to rob. That was when Old Kat would throw the bucket.

When the tide turned, the current usually carried the ships past the black rock and beached them where Old Kat had a nice sideline in chariot hire and travel guides.

"Have you forgotten everything your dear daddy taught you?" asked Old Kat. "Never sail lee side of hidden rocks when the fog is up."

"Blast that, there's no time for it," growled our

Captain. "We took a lightning strike on the mast. Now she's swallowing water like a dog in summer."

"You! Old pirate! Have your crew carry my luggage to your ship. Be quick about it and you will be rewarded," said Narkittus.

"I expect I will, but who in Neptuna's name might you be?" laughed Old Kat.

"My name is Narkittus. I am the Emperor's assistant. You would do well to remember that."

"A cat of noble birth," laughed Old Kat. "What a beautiful catch! I'll bet there's a great reward for rescuing one so close to the Emperor. Put him aboard and careful with his luggage – there might be valuables in it."

"Father!" said Captain Kat.

"What was that reward you were talking about, Your Highness?" asked Old Kat.

"We will speak of that in private, when I am on board your ship," said Narkittus.

"We will speak of it now, Your Highness" growled the old pirate. "And I'd speak up quick if I were you, for we're half sunk already by the sound of it."

The ship's timbers began to creak and split and the deck was sloping.

"Listen to me," said Narkittus. "I need to buy passage to the Land of the Kitons. You will take me there. You are all skin and bone but you have lived to a ripe old age. If you wish to live much longer, you will order your crew not to meddle with my luggage.

Death will come to the one who opens that box. Tell your crew that."

There was a chill in these words and for a moment all fell silent.

"His crew?" laughed Captain Kat. "I suppose you mean the CUT-THROAT PIRATES? There's just him and a couple of drunkards aboard, I'll bet."

Just then there was a lurch as the ship's prow began to rise. The water had got in below decks and she was sinking fast.

"Shake your tails or you'll be sailing a wreck!" cried Old Kat.

Just as the last of us were aboard, our poor ship slipped under the waves.

Old Kat's ship was also named The Stroker – it being a tradition in the Kat family to give all of their ships this name. Whether this was to bring good fortune or to avoid taxes, I have no clue. Although it has not proved to be a lucky tradition, for I am told that out of seven previous Strokers: three were sunk on rocks; three were set alight by accident; and the last one was scuttled so that a large claim could be made on an insurance policy arranged with a Squeak banker. Perhaps it is no surprise that Captain Kat was not confident about Narkittus's plan to give Old Kat the job of navigator.

"Navigate to the Land of the Kitons?" he laughed. "Father's lucky if he can navigate back to his own basket every night."

And so Captain Kat was hired as a navigator and his crew were kept on too. Narkittus insisted that the mate who had tried to start the mutiny was put ashore.

Narkittus is full of surprises. I asked Captain Kat if his father had got a good price for our transport and he smiled. Narkittus had bought the ship itself – for three times its true value – and doubled the crew's wages.

"That is unusually generous of Narkittus. In Rome he is famous for his short paws and long pockets," I said.

"Generous?" growled the Captain. "As soon as the crew found out where they were going, they wanted danger money. For that land is wild."

MAIUS XXIX

May 29th

A Present from the Captain

NEWS OF GREAT importance! Today Captain Kat told me of Narkittus's plan. Our ship will meet up with with General Mawlus and the fleet before the invasion is launched. Having guessed of my interest in the Land of the Kitons, he brought out a book for me – "to help you pass the long hours," he said.

I was longing for some excitement. I know that this

may sound hard to believe after all I have been through, but on board ship the days are long. Sometimes a rat with a limp is the most interesting sight you'll see all day. I unwrapped the bundle and read:

The Diary of Mewlius Caesar

Mewlius Caesar is known to every Roman kitten. Tales of his heroic deeds add a dash of danger to our comfortable firesides. He sailed to the Land of the Kitons and returned to tell the tale. He did this not once but three times! Even though this was one hundred years ago, our young still remember him and love to play fight with a good game of 'Caesar and Kitons". I lost every one of these play fights of course. On account of my ginger coat I was always chosen to play the Kiton. And Caesar always tramples upon the savage Kitons when he conquers them, so it is said. I paused for a moment, remembering those tramplings that made the happiest days of my life so miserable.

Finally, I said "Thank you Captain. I am delighted. Is it a good read?"

"I cannot say for sure," answered Kat, "for I never got past the first chapter. He loves the sound of his own voice. But what I did read confirmed my thoughts about Mewlius Caesar."

"That he was the greatest soldier that Rome has ever known?" I asked.

"That he was the greatest fool Rome has ever

known!" he answered. "His first invasion was a disaster. The troops got off the boat and the sun was shining. Mewlius thought his navigator had landed him in Maul!"

That was the one and only day of Kittish summer.

"But he came back. He tried again," I said trying to remember my history lessons.

"You have to admire him for not giving up."

"He had a big mouth and no sense. Launched his second invasion at low tide. His troops were miles away from the beach when they landed. They struggled through the mud while the Kiton warriors picked them off with arrows from a safe distance."

"I see," I replied. "I don't remember ever hearing it told like that before."

"You won't find that in the history books. That's something my grandfather told me. And he should know, he was there."

"Your grandfather fought with Mewlius at the invasion?" I asked.

"Not quite. He was with the other lot," said Kat.

"He was a Kiton warrior?" I gasped. I could not believe that Kat's family were descended from the Kitons. I wanted to tell him that I also have Kiton blood, but something held my tongue.

"He was a trader, not a warrior. Rome's been trading with the Kitons for centuries. Peus knows why we need to go invading them now."

Kat padded softly towards the cabin door.

"Captain," I said, "tell me, if your family are Kitons, why did you get involved in the invasion?"

"Narkittus chartered the ship to go to Maul, not the Land of the Kitons. The first I heard of the invasion was when he made that offer to my father." Then he lowered his voice to a whisper and continued. "This will be a bloody business. Gold or no, I wish I had no part of it."

"General Mawlus has four legions, armed to the teeth. I hardly think the Kitons have a chance," I said.

"A word of warning Spartapuss, if there's one thing the Kitons hate it's a turntail."

"A turntail?" I asked.

"A Kiton who has betrayed their tribe and gone over to another tribe. Or worse still, to the Roman invaders. For a Kiton, a turntail is worse than an enemy. Remember that."

THE DIARY OF MEWLIUS CAESAR

Of the Land of the Kitons

I, Caesar, have seen this land three times, with my own eyes. It is green yet most unpleasant. The rain is constant and the rivers are full of crocodiles that can snap a cow in half with their enormous snouts.

There is some silver in the green hills to the west and south west and there is rich farmland. Sadly, the Kitons themselves are the very worst savages, beyond any hope of taming. They have a saying that 'Kitons never, never, never will be slaves.' This is a good thing because they would only be fit to make slaves of the very lowest order. They cannot write, which means they are not fit to be sold as teachers or scribes, like the Squeaks. They cannot sing like the Fleagyptians. They howl so horribly that the best of them could not carry a tune in a bucket. With so many slaves on the market these days, it would hardly be worth the expense of transporting them to Rome, for they would not fetch a good price at auction. Some of their warriors are skilled with the battle chariot and may be sold as gladiators but that is about all they are good for.

MEWNONIUS I

(June 1st)

I NEVER WANTED TO come on this voyage. But now I am here, I thought that I could do my duty as a Roman and see my ancestor's home for the first time. Now the Captain tells me that I will be greeted as a traitor and a 'turntail' because I look like a Kiton but have the voice and manners of a Roman. At least it will be over soon. The wind has picked up and we are making good progress. We should be on time for our meeting with General Mawlus. Today we saw another ship. The Captain says it was flying Roman colours. Perhaps this was the first in the fleet.

A second entry in this diary today. I was most surprised when Narkittus called me to a meeting in the Captain's cabin. When I arrived neither Kat, Old or Young, was there. When I padded in, Narkittus was pouring over some charts. We had been on board two ships together now for six weeks and at last he said his first words to me.

"I am going to attend a conference of war on board General Mawlus" flagship tomorrow. You are coming with me."

I was about to make some excuse when he added:

"By order of Clawdius, Caesar Best and Greatest, you are to report to me directly."

MEWNONIUS II

(June 2nd)

On The General's Ship

As we tied up alongside the flagship, my stomach was in my mouth. Whether this was out of fear of General Mawlus or because of the waves, I do not know. It is said that General Mawlus hates all of the Emperor's advisers – especially our Squeak friend. If that was not true before we arrived, it was certainly true after we left.

On arrival, we were escorted to a room deep in the belly of the ship where General Mawlus and his second in command, Vespurrsian were looking over pile of charts.

"The Emperor's assistant is here," said Vespurrsian, who was sharpening his elegant claws with a silver file. He looked more of an athlete than a hardened fighter.

"I can smell him," sighed Mawlus without looking up from the map.

"You're late," said Vespurrsian. "But you haven't missed much. Just tactics and such."

Mawlus sighed. What were they teaching them at the academy these days? Advanced training in stating the obvious?

"General, where will our fleet land? I want a full report," said Narkittus.

"That is a military matter. We'll let you know when the time is right," growled Mawlus.

"Have you forgotten that I was sent by your commander in chief? Your Emperor?" said Mawlus. "He hears what I hear, and he is very interested in tactics."

"Take him through it," ordered Mawlus. Vespurrsian put down his claw file and began. The young lieutenant was thought to be one of the most promising fighters in the army, but he wasn't used to speech making. "Um... Well... we haven't decided for certain. But we're thinking of landing on two different beaches."

"Why?" asked General Mawlus.

"In order to confuse the enemy sir?" asked Vespurrsian.

"In the Roman army we learn from our mistakes," said Mawlus in a weary voice. "Landing on two beaches rather than one commits the enemy to defend two places and weakens their force by half."

"Who commands the Kitons?" asked Narkittus.

"Our spies report that their leaders are two princes. Characterpuss and his brother Todo... To-do puss ..."

"Todimpuss. And his brother Carac-tapuss," said Narkittus.

"Carac-tapuss?" asked General Mawlus.

Narkittus nodded.

"These Kitons have savagely difficult names don't they?" said Vespurrsian. "We're calling them Carac and TDP for short. One is smart but the other one is as dull as a Squeak's sword. No offence meant, Narkittus."

"Really?" said Narkittus. "And which is which?"

"Our intelligence isn't that clear,' said Vespurrsian.

I later learned that Todimpuss had been nicknamed 'Too dumb puss' as he was thought to lack the brains to rule his tribe. These two Kiton leaders were set against General Mawlus and Vespurrsian.

"We will follow in the example of the great Mewlius Caesar and land here and here," said Vespurrsian, pointing at the map.

I said nothing, wondering if they'd get the tides right this time. I feared getting stuck in the freezing mud more than I feared the Kitons.

"Are you expecting heavy opposition?" asked Narkittus.

"The usual. Their warriors will be supported by a rabble. An army of farmers with clubs and sickles – that sort of thing. We're expecting a good turnout because it's the fighting season. Every year in the month of Maius the tribes like to feast for a few days and come down to the beaches to fight each other. We have no idea why."

"It's traditional around here," said Narkittus. "Be warned General. If you are expecting a beach party or a brawl with a rabble, you are mistaken. These Kitons fight like the heroes of old, in chariots. Each chariot fighter is supported by two warriors armed with axes and broadswords. They are not as disciplined as

Romans but they train their young to fight before their eyes are open. You had best be prepared for it."

"Spare us your lecture, Squeak," said General Mawlus.

Narkittus padded towards the door, without another word.

"One more thing Narkittus, the Womps are to be put on board my ship."

"Impossible," said Narkittus.

"You are the representative of the Emperor. Don't we all know it? You never tire of reminding us. But here is an order, signed by Clawdius himself, authorising that all magical weapons be handed over to the battlefield commander."

"Still impossible," said Narkittus. "The weapons were lost when our first ship went down."

"What a pity," said Vespurrsian.

Mawlus searched for a lie in Narkittus's eyes, holding his gaze before finally letting out a low hiss: "Well adviser, thanks for your help. It appears that your schemes have come to nothing. When magic fails, Roman claws and steel must do the job."

MEWNONIUS III

(June 3rd)

Of Speeches and Beaches

IT IS THE EVE OF the invasion and the Generals are looking forward to a bloody struggle. They have given us one already in the form of their traditional 'eve of battle' speeches. Mawlus talked tactics in a flat voice. It was all that I could do not to let out a yawn. Narkittus read out a message from the Emperor but his booming voice only drew laughter from the ranks.

We are told that The Kitons are savages who will spit hate at any invader who dares enter their territory. But they are not my main worry.

For last night, Narkittus told General Mawlus that the Weapons of Magical Power went down with our first ship. But this cannot be true – for I saw his crate loaded onto Old Kat's ship with my own eyes. I fear that I may have seen too much. I am now the only witness to Narkittus's lie, a dangerous position to be in. For it stands to reason that no one makes it to high office in the Imperial Palace without a little blood on their paws. I have resolved to watch my back.

THE DIARY OF MEWLIUS CAESAR

Of *The Mewids and their*
Strange and Savage Ways

THE VERY WORST amongst this savage land are the priests, who are called the Mewids. Little is known of the Mewids' religion, for they keep the names of their gods secret and it is death to speak of them. The Mewid religion has spread like a sickness throughout the tribes of that backward land and across the sea to the land of Maul. Every forest in the land has a grove of oak trees where Mewids in white robes meet in secret and light the fires of sacrifice. They must be stopped as soon as we have enough soldiers to drive them from their hiding places in the dark woods.

MEWNONIUS IV
(June 4th)

MY HEART WAS out of my mouth this morning as I leapt into the landing boat in the half-light. As I made the leap, the waves drew the boat away from the side of the ship and I feared that I'd be the first casualty of this invasion. As Fortune willed it, Captain Kat was in charge of our boat and he managed to drag me on board so I escaped with only a soaking of the back legs. We are to go with General Mawlus, whilst

Narkittus goes with Vespurrsian's force. There is little love lost between our Squeak friend and the General. Having seen the map, Kat thought that our beach was the better of the two landing places. The Kitons will be ready for us, but there is some cover in the rocks and the slope of the beach is easier. We do not want to be caught in the mud when they come at us.

The landing boat struggled through the surf, sitting low in the water. It was heavily loaded as the troops were armed to the teeth. After a few minutes we saw white cliffs peeping like ghosts through the mist. Then the rain began to fall. I have never known rain so cold. I thought of the afterlife. It is said that the gods return you to your true home after your death. I wondered if they might make an exception in my case, for this land of my ancestors looked every bit as bleak as Narkittus had said.

We made no noise as we struggled ashore and formed up into our positions. Mawlus had told us to expect clouds of arrows to soften us and stop us from moving up the beach. And then the famous chariot charge. So we peered through the mist and shivered, each of us thinking the same thing.

"Where are the Kitons?" I asked.

"Not here," said Captain Kat.

There is an old Kiton rhyme that goes:

Rain, rain
Leave me be
Fall upon my enemy

Perhaps our enemies had been singing this, for the reports from the other landing place were the same. The Kitons, it seemed, had decided not to fight us on the beaches. Not today at any rate. There was not a sniff of a Kiton – nor any bird or living thing in the countryside for miles around. Not even the sun had come out to meet us.

MEWNONIUS V

(June 5th)

A New Dawn Brings More Rain

A NEW MORNING brought new rain. This time it blew around like mist. There were more arguments about where to find the enemy. Some say that General Mawlus will attack their stronghold at Camulod.

Kat and I shared our breakfast with a couple of slingers. Kat was careful to keep his boat in sight at all times.

"Hey Captain, you've been in this dump before. Have you any idea where the Kitons are hiding?" asked one of the slingers, searching for stones in the sand.

"No idea," said Kat. "I was hired to get you lot

safely onto the beach and not a step further."

"I heard we were going inland to where the friend-lies have their camp," said the second slinger.

"The friendlies?" I said "That's a nice name for a tribe."

The slingers began to shake with laughter.

"The friendlies isn't a tribe," said Kat. "There are two tribes friendly to Rome as far as I know. And they're called the Micini and the Catrebates – or the Catres for short. We're in their territory now. The Romans call them friendlies."

"Well at least there's some hope for peace in this land – if Mice and Cats can live side by side," I said, feeling rather pleased with my joke.

"They hate each other," said Kat. "They've only joined forces with Rome because they're afraid of Todimpuss and Carac, of the Catu tribe."

"I see," I replied, but in truth it was far from clear. It was another strange Kiton name to add to the list. I had thought of my homeland as a simple place, close to nature and free from the scandal of Rome. The sort of place that they sing about in songs. 'Oh Brown Fields of my Fathers' and that sort of thing. But even the simple places are complicated these days. With all these tribes about, I was struggling to keep up.

It seemed that our Commanders were doing little better, for it was late afternoon before they had made their minds up. But at last we set off inland in a north-easterly direction. I was surprised to find that Captain

Kat was coming with us.

"I thought you were staying with the ship," I said.

"I couldn't leave my shipmate to go straying all over the place," laughed Kat. "Besides, Narkittus has made me an offer."

Before I could find out more, the head of our line halted at the top of the cliff and there was a crush in the ranks.

"Come on, let's take a look," said Kat, pushing his way along the lines to the front of the column. When we arrived, we found that the march had been stopped so that our leaders could examine a wooden post. There were fresh scratch marks at the bottom, made by big claws, and there was ginger fur all around.

"Don't look at me, I'm not shedding!" I said.

"What do you make of this?" asked the Scenturion in charge.

"It's a message, to trespassers from other tribes," said Captain Kat.

"Can you read it?" asked the Scenturion. I must admit I was pleased to have a friend like Kat along.

"There's nothing to read," said Kat. "It's a warning – 'Keep off Our Land!'"

We were entering hostile country. A report was sent to General Mawlus immediately.

The ground became easier as the country flattened out. The rain was still cold and miserable but I noticed for the first time that the land was very green. Light green pastures and dark green trees. Green has never been my favourite colour. But I had to admit there was beauty in this wilderness. I have never liked the countryside, being very much a city cat who gets alarmed when I go more than five minutes away from a fish shop. Now I was 'making camp' which meant hunting for a dry sleeping place and breaking out the ship's biscuits (which had not been softened by the constant rain). If this was not the middle of nowhere, it was somewhere close.

MEWNONIUS VI

(June 6th)

A Stand Stone

WHEN I HAULED myself up for breakfast, my pads were red as a butcher's slab. It must have been those sharp stones on the cliff path. Captain Kat didn't look much better. I asked him if he was well rested.

"I didn't sleep a wink," he said. "I never do when I get onto dry land. It's too still for my liking."

We shared breakfast with the slingers, who had managed to get a fire going, and then struck camp. Soon we were marching again through country that was green but empty, save for the occasional 'hag tree', as the locals call them. But where were the locals? There was no sign of anyone – friendly or fierce. It was nearing lunchtime and I was wondering whether, if we did come across a friendly village, I might be able to buy a roast chicken. Kat says that the friendlies will accept our money, although they have been making their own coins since before the times of Mewlious. We sold them the moulds to do the minting, but some of their early efforts were a bit basic – the head of their local chief stuck onto the body of Hercatules, for example.

I was thinking of this when our column came to a sudden halt. Once again, Kat and I moved up the lines to get a look at what was happening. By the side of the path stood a tall grey stone, very like the block of a great statue, but before the carvers have started. Why anyone would go to the trouble of placing it there, I cannot say. There were scorches at the base of the stone, and the embers of a small fire were visible. The smell of wild herbs filled the air.

Kat stopped still and his ears went up.

"What is it?" I asked. I turned a slow circle and had a careful look around. But there was nothing. Only wet grass in another shade of green.

"You won't see them unless they want to be seen," said Kat. "But you might hear them calling."

The order came to move on but Kat and I held back and let the others go ahead. We were not the only ones hanging back.

"It's pointless," groaned a tattered soldier, who

looked far too old for this campaign.

"It's orders, Ruffus," the other replied.

"There's a lot of orders in the army lad," said Ruffus. "An' if I'd followed 'em all, I'd be under a slab by now, cold in the ground. Mind you, at least I'd be dry."

"These orders come from the Emperor himself," said Furbius. "Destroy all Mewid shrines, groves, altars, barrows and stand stones."

"This don't look like sand stone to me – looks more like granite," said Ruffus.

"Get on with it," sighed the other.

"Pulling down a dirty great stone ain't gonna 'elp. They can easily stand it back up again when we've gone. Besides we ain't got no workshop. Where are we going to get a block and tackle?"

"You could hit it with yer 'ammer,' suggested a third.

"I'll 'ammer you in a moment," said Ruffus.

"Mewids!" I said. "Are we in Mewid country now?"

"This whole land is Mewid country," laughed Kat, pointing at the scorch marks around the base of the stone. "Burning that offering is their way of letting us know they're here."

"What's a stand stone?" I asked.

But before he could answer, I was almost run down by a chariot that came screaming out of nowhere. It was a four-dog rig, and the lead dog aimed a bite at me as they tore past.

"Out the way Catre scum!" spat the driver.

"What did he call me?"

"Scum, weren't it?" said Kat.

"Yes but what was the other bit about?"

"The Catres – The Ginger Ones, remember?"

"So he mistook me for a Catre?" I asked.

"Looks like it. He was a Micini by the look of it. Welcome home Spartapuss," said Captain Kat.

I cleaned the mud from my face and tried to make sense of it. At last I said:

"But if he's a Kiton warrior, why don't those soldiers stop hammering at that stone and get after him?" I asked.

"You're not the fastest ship in the fleet are you?" said Kat. "He's a friendly, from the Micini tribe. A messenger most likely. They hate the Catre tribe. That's why he spat at you."

"How can you tell he's Micini?" I asked.

"From the blue stain on his collar," said Kat.

"Is that the 'war paint' that they are famous for wearing in battle?" I asked.

"No," replied Kat. "The Micini have probably just been painting their fences. But he's one of them all right. The Micini tend to have a hungry look, as if they never get enough breakfast."

"And the Micini have gone over to the side of the Romans?" I asked.

"That's about the cut of it," said Kat with a chuckle.

I did not see the funny side. The Roman slingers had mocked me for my Kiton colouring, but the first Kiton I met had tried to run me down for looking like a member of a rival tribe.

Kat decided that we should follow the messenger and catch up with the rest of the legion. It was a hard march but we made good progress.

As night fell we caught up with our slinger friends. Kat brought out some more ship's biscuits, which we swapped for a taste of their meat stew.

It wasn't long before word got out that Vespurrsian's scouts had got scent of the enemy. They were thought to be hiding in the trackless marshes to the east.

"Marshes," moaned a slinger. "Better stock up on stones now lads, if you want to keep your paws dry. I don't fancy grubbing around in that marsh mud. You don't know what's down there."

Slingers are obsessed with the collection of stones and when they are not collecting stones they are swapping them or hoarding them or stealing them from other slingers. Still it is better to be a slinger than a front line fighter. Although it is less heroic – why run to danger when you can taunt the enemy from a safe distance with stones and darts? Clawdius himself had ordered extra slingers for the campaign, as the Kitons' chariot dogs are to be their targets.

Tomorrow we will join with Vespurrsian's force. For it is the Roman fighting way to assemble the largest possible force before an attack.

"That's because your generals like a big audience for their speeches," said Kat.

MEWNONIUS X

(June 10th)

With The Mewids

THIS LAND GROWS stranger and stranger. The locals are amazed by the simplest acts. They have never seen anyone writing before. They insist that I must give them a demonstration of the scribe's art. I have agreed, on the condition that they do not tell their teachers. After I have finished writing my account, I have promised to read it out to them.

"It will take a while," I said, "for it has been ten days since the great battle and there is much to tell, mostly rain and different shades of green. Do you want a short version?"

"Leave nothing out!" they cried. "In this land our stories take days to tell, and even then they don't get to the point."

So I shall do as they ask and explain how I came to this most unusual place.

KITON HUNT

So it was that we were going on a 'Kiton hunt', as Mawlus called it in his speech. I admit that I was not looking forward to it. On the way towards the marshes we moved from the open land into woods, all tangled with undergrowth or overgrowth – I cannot say which. The general had now met with his Kiton guide, who led us to a narrow track just wide enough for one chariot, so we had to march in single file. Any delay up ahead would cause the line to stop. After three hours of this stop-start marching, tempers were getting short.

"Can we not go by a road instead of this rabbit track?" I moaned, after snagging my claw on a tree root for the second time that morning.

"This is a road," laughed Kat. "It's the oldest road in the country. Kitons have been coming down here since time began. In fact the Catre call it "main road" in their tongue. They are rather proud of it. It's been widened twice and there's talk of putting a toll gate at each end of it."

"If they'd chopped down a few trees and built it straight in the first place, we'd get there much quicker."

"The forest is old too," said Kat. "Those oaks have stood for six hundred years. Why chop them down, when you can go around?"

Just as we were talking we came to a little side-track, no more than a hole in the tall grass, to the side of the track. Kat motioned to me to follow.

"What in Peus's name is down there?" I asked.

"It is called a "fasttrack". It's for overtaking if there's a slow cart or suchlike ahead," answered Kat.

And so it proved. In less than an hour's time, as my thoughts were turning to lunch, the trees came to a sudden end. We came out of the woods and stood at the edge of a high bank, looking down upon a wide river. Assembled just five hundred tails away, on the opposite bank, was the most unruly army I have ever seen. Tents of many different types and colours were pitched in a rather careless fashion. They didn't seem to be formed up in any order. Chariot dogs were sniffing around all over the place – half of them weren't tied up properly. Smoke from great cooking fires rose up and mingled with the mist. These Kitons seemed to be out for a spring picnic, rather than a battle. The first thing that a Roman does when he makes camp is to pitch his tent at the end of an orderly row, then build up some defences such as sharpened posts to guard against an attack. Whereas the first thing that a Kiton does when he makes camp is get a large fire going, brew up some herbs with hot water and roast the biggest piece of meat he can find, until it is charred black. Only when he and his dog have had their fill, will he think about pitching his tent. By this time it will be too dark to find the tent pegs.

"Look! It's starting," said Kat.

Already the first of Mawlus's legions were emerging from the woods on our side of the river and forming up into neat squares. They were in plain sight of the Kitons, who didn't seem to care. They padded about their camp at a leisurely pace, more intent on roasting their chickens than readying themselves for battle. Whether this was due to bravery or stupidity, I cannot say. I had to feel sorry for the Kitons. This was going to be a massacre.

"Are they blind?" I said. "Can't they see that General Mawlus is coming? You can't miss him. He's the one with the great golden eagle on the pole."

"They can see him," Kat replied sadly.

"So why are they just lying around over there? Why don't they do something?"

Before Kat had a chance to answer, the whiskers on my right side gave a twinge. As I turned I saw the chariot coming fast towards me.

"Run!" hissed Kat - diving into the trees and tearing a path through the undergrowth where the chariot could not follow.

I'd started to run when I was seized and hoisted up by the collar. I now sat whisker to whisker with two Kiton warriors, who for the tale's sake I shall call Howl and Gruff.

I have not spoken the tongue of the Kitons since I was very young and I only know my tribe's dialect. I can only guess what these two were saying but, for the sake of a complete story of these great events, I will follow the example of the great philosopher Cato who says that where history is hidden, the trick is to make up something suitable, for the good of the tale.

"Whoa Ginger," said Howl, in a rolling voice. "Watch where you're going! You're running straight towards the camp of the snail eaters!"

"You're all the same, you Catres - six claws but half a brain," said Gruff, slowing the dogs to a trot and spinning the chariot around effortlessly.

"Still – you makes up for it when it comes to a fight eh?" said Howl.

"Don't we get a thank you or nothing?" asked Gruff.

Not knowing what to say, I replied as best I could with the words 'thank you' in my tribe's tongue and that seemed to be good enough.

The chariot was small – more like a racing rig than a battle chariot. And the dogs had a lean and hungry look. But it was fast. In a flash we were down by the banks of the wide river.

"Your boat or mine Ginger?" asked Gruff with a smile, although he knew that he would get no sense out of me. "Looks like it's mine then."

He found the spot where he'd hidden his boat we soon crossed the river with the dogs swimming alongside.

From the Kiton's side of the river, the Romans were

in plain view. I could see the banners of the XI Legion flying in the breeze. They were moving down the slope and taking positions by the banks. But the Kitons did not seem to notice. Either they had no fear, or they did not expect an attack. Perhaps they did not understand Roman tactics, or they were just foolish. I feared this last case must be most likely, for up close, the Kiton's camp looked a terrible mess. Tents were pitched everywhere and chariot dogs fought over bones.

My 'rescuers' made sure I kept close as they picked a weaving path through the cluttered camp, from the riverbank up to higher ground. Once I tried to slip off, only to feel Gruff's paw on my shoulder. He pointed towards the tree line.

"Don't get lost. We're meeting at the Lightning Oak," he said. "Everyone's up there already."

As we pushed through the crowds I became aware that this was a public meeting – something like our Senate at Rome, only held in woods.

An important Kiton was speaking. I was soon to find out that this was none other than Carac – one of the two Kiton Princes who stood against Mawlus and Vespurrsian. He was sitting on the trunk of a fallen oak. Lightning had split the tree in two and sent it crashing down against a great boulder. Now the great trunk made a perfect speaker's platform.

"Friends, I have said enough. Tomorrow will be ours

if the Great Mother wills it. Return to your clans and be ready," said Carac.

Peus be thanked, I thought to myself, realising that I had arrived at the end of the speech.

Just then a thin voice hissed.

"Where are your Ginger friends now, great Prince of the Kitons? Curse the Turntails. They've sold us all to the Romans, or my dear mother is a she-wolf."

"Haven't you got enough enemies to fight, Brother of the Rocks?" said Carac. "I beg you, leave the Catres to me. I still hope they can be persuaded to join us. Besides my friends, there are Romans aplenty out there for us. We need new friends, not more enemies."

A part of the crowd was not satisfied with this. There were shouts of "Death to the Gingers! Death to the turntails!"

"You cannot play me like my mother's harp!" spat the Chief (who must have been most fond of his mother). "Even here in this council you shield your Catre friends while they plot in front of our noses."

As he spoke I felt many eyes upon me.

"Death to the turntails!" shouted a voice.

"Death to the gingers!" shouted another.

"Turntail! Turntail!" spat the thin voice.

For Peus's sake, I thought, here we go again!

MISTAKEN FOR A CATRE

As I was shoved into the centre of the throng I cried "You've got it wrong!" There is a wildness about any crowd fed by the prospect of a blood fight. Soon it was a turning circle, hissing and spitting. They would tear me apart, piece by piece, if they were not stopped. Using all my strength I leapt up onto the Lightning Oak. The crowd seethed below me.

"You left that a bit late my Catre friend," said Carac. He seemed pleased that I had joined him on the lightning tree.

"I am not a Catre," I replied, "I am Spartapuss."

"Hear me! Hear me!" called Carac in a great voice. "A challenge has been issued. This Spartapuss of the, er ... What was your tribe?"

Without waiting for my answer he continued. "This Spartapuss now challenges Tomuss of the Sillures tribe to single combat."

"No I do not!" I gasped. Carac gave me a hard stare. "I mean, I didn't mean to. I'm sure we could all work this out."

The next thing I saw was a spitting ball of hate. Tomuss sprung from the midst of the crowd like a shot from a sling. His right claw caught me on the ear as I backed away and it was all I could do to avoid a fall. And to fall under the claws of the mob below me was to fall into the underworld itself. I tried to remember my gladiator training, but there was no sand in this arena. Oh Tefnut! How I needed her now.

Tomuss came at me again. This time he disguised his attack. He spun around and rolled over me, trying to get a good bite on my neck. My collar saved me from serious hurt and I was able to shake him off. Suddenly all was still. I felt very calm as I began the dance. A short leap forward, shift left, shift right and roll. Sweep with the tail. I stumbled as if to fall, as I turned myself around in mid air. I'd give these Kitons a lesson in the martial arts. I was sure that they'd never seen anything like this before! And then a crash. I'd totally missed the landing and was hanging on by the slightest claw to a thin twig on the underside of the branch.

Tomuss, who had been taken by surprise, now yowled in rage searching everywhere for me. The crowd thought this was the funniest thing they'd ever seen. A warrior of the rocks fooled by a disappearing Catre!

"Show yourself!" spat Tomuss. The crowd laughed again.

I must admit that I mugged up to this by putting a paw over my mouth and telling them to "sssh" in the manner of a bad actor at one of the Arena sideshows.

Poor Tomuss was driven mad by their behaviour. He prowled from one edge of the trunk to the other, like a bear on a chain. But he could see no sign of me.

I did not trust the crowd, for I knew only too well that they could turn at any minute, so I chose my moment. When he had made a pass I swung myself up, right in front of his face and gave his whiskers a strong pull. It was too much; in his heavy armour he began to lose his balance. He dropped like a felled oak into the throng below.

"Turntail!" hissed my enemy from the pit. He was ready to come at me again.

"Enough!" said Carac. "You know the law Tomuss. You can't challenge him twice this day."

"Death to the Catres!" spat Tomuss. The shouts were taken up by some of his supporters.

"I am not a Catre," I called.

"Enough!" said Carac. "Save it for the Romans. Go back to your clans and make ready." And then in a lower voice he asked "What is your clan Spartapuss?"

"I don't have a clan. Not here at any rate. I'm not from around these parts," I replied.

"That we can tell from your speech," said Carac.

"I thought he was a Micini at first Chief," said Gruff. "One of my sister's lot - they swore they'd stand shoulder to shoulder with us."

"Micini scum! They'd be late for their own funerals," said Howl. "I'd rather not stand shoulder to shoulder with them, they stink of bad meat."

"They've gone over to the Romans," said Carac quietly. "But anyway Spartapuss, you are not being entirely honest with me. You will remain with us until after the battle. Then we will speak."

"Thank you Prince Carac. But may I ask one thing? The clans do not seem to be prepared for the battle. General Mawlus is already…"

I stopped, for fear that I would say too much. There

was something strange about Carac. I felt I could trust him, although he was the enemy of Rome.

"Go on," he said quietly.

"Aren't you worried that General Mawlus will attack before tomorrow?"

"How can he?" said Carac. "The river stands between us and he has no boats. Our spies are quite certain of that."

I was speechless! This Prince of the Kitons had been trained in battle tactics from the litter yet he could not imagine that the Romans might swim across the river, or build a bridge. For cats here cannot stand the water – the thought of swimming is completely against their nature. And they do not take their builders with them when they go on campaign. For in this land, it is impossible to get a builder to turn up on time.

My flicking tail gave me away.

"You think they'll get across," said Carac. "You know a lot about Romans, don't you Spartapuss?"

"We picked him up by the Roman lines," said Gruff. "Do you think he's a spy?"

"I must go," said Carac. "Take him to the stronghold. Be sure no harm comes to him."

A WALK IN THE DARK

I was blindfolded and marched away. It was a while before that blindfold was taken off. I remember the smell - earthy and damp. They gave me a drink but I fear it was drugged for, when I awoke, I had a thumping headache. A spikey-tailed tabby entered and began to laugh. I wondered what it was about jailers. Did the job appeal to a certain type of twisted personality? Did they seek out the job or were they chosen for it?

"Wakey wakey!" said the jailer cheerfully. I was happier when they were shouting at you. When the jailers were smiling was when you knew they had something nasty in mind.

"Did you have sweet dreams ginger?" purred the jailer softly.

Here we go – it's coming now, I thought.

"Wake up turntail!" spat the jailer. "You're wanted for questioning."

"Does Prince Carac want to ask me some more questions?" I said, trying to sound casual.

"Carac?" said the jailer, "he's a right Prince. He probably even told them not to let us hurt you, didn't he?"

As he stalked around the cell, the whiskers on my right side gave a shiver.

"Thing is, Prince Carac is busy chasing your Roman friends, so his little brother is going to ask the questions."

"His brother?" I asked.

"You've never known two brothers so unlike each other. It's uncanny that they came from the same litter."

"I see," I said, not liking where this was going.

"Carac, for example - he can't bear to see torture. It makes him break down and weep. But he does it anyway, for the good of the tribe. Only he looks away during the bad bits. But his brother, now he's a different piece of work."

The jailer left a long pause. I tried to tell myself that he'd done this routine many times before. But it was no good, it was working on me.

"A word of advice," said Tabby, finally. "If you've got anything to say to young Dimpuss, you'd better spit it out quick while you've still got a mouth to spit from."

THE BAD PRINCE

So I was taken for questioning by Todimpuss, the same prince of the Kitons whose letter to Clawdius, demanding the return of the Womps, had started all this. It is said that before you die, a series of strange thoughts flash through your mind. Perhaps it is the same with torture. For some reason I remembered Todimpuss had started his letter "To the idiot Clawdius." That had made the whole city laugh. I wondered what they were laughing at now.

"Anything to say before you die, turntail?" asked the jailer, pleasantly.

"I'm not a turntail," I replied.

"I'll be the judge of that!" growled another voice. It was Todimpuss.

What's the use? I thought. They're going to get it out of me anyway. It wasn't long before the jailer began his routine.

"By the law of the Clans, the punishment for being a turntail is…"

"Death," hissed Todimpuss. "Death take all who turn their backs on their tribes. Death comes on swift wings to those who stand with the invaders."

"Well I'm not a turntail. I can't be, because I'm half Roman."

"Roman?" came a low growl.

"Shall I show him what we do to Romans, Chief?"

I heard a growl, which I took for a "Yes".

I was dragged from the cell and up a damp tunnel. Finally, my blindfold was pulled down and I stood blinking in the weak light of the afternoon sun. The rain still hadn't stopped but we were sheltered by the branches high above us. We were on a forest track. In front of me, two chariots were lined up facing in opposite directions. Tied in between the chariots was a crude model dressed in Roman clothing. It was stuffed with straw.

"Witness the punishment for being a Roman in this land," said the tabby. At a signal from Todimpuss the chariots began to race away from each other. There was a crack of ropes tightening and the Roman's 'tail' was torn off. Both halves of the dummy were dragged down the track at a frightening speed. By the time the chariots were back in their positions, only the head and torn tail of the dummy were left.

"I'm half Roman," I said.

"So is that," said the tabby, pointing at the model.

I now took the place of the dummy, which had had its stuffing torn out.

"Wait! I'll talk," I said.

"Of course you will," laughed the tabby. "You all do!" Then turning to Todimpuss he said, "Shall I send for a Mewid, Chief?"

"No!" spat the Prince in a rage.

"Don't you think we better had, Chief?" asked the jailer.

"No!" growled the chief, they meddle. Whatever we learn they will know soon enough."

Todimpuss padded up, very close. He was no 'Best in Show' and didn't look much like his sleek brother.

"So half-breed, what can you tell us? I heard a whisper that the Roman King is coming to our land. Tell me where I find him and I will give you an easier death."

I was amazed. Not even the Romans were supposed to know of Clawdius's arrival.

"Clawdius won't come until it is safe," I replied.

"Coward!" hissed Todimpuss. "He brings shame to his clan. Why do they allow themselves to be ruled by such a one?"

"He's not that bad," I said. "You should have seen Catligula, the last Emperor."

"He is gutless," said Todimpuss.

"You'll be gutless soon, turntail," said the tabby as

he checked my ropes. "Your ride is here."

Todimpuss motioned to the charioteers to make ready.

"No please!" I begged.

"Your chariot awaits!" grinned the Tabby.

"Stop! I said. I'll tell you about the Womps."

"Womps?" asked Todimpuss, turning his head to one side.

"The magical weapons. The ones you asked for in your letter to Clawdius," I gasped.

Todimpuss flicked his tail and turned his head to the side again.

"Letter?" he asked.

"About the Weapons of Magical Power. Someone stole them and you wanted them back. Remember?"

The tabby pulled the rope around my collar tight.

"Vericat! Vericat stole them!" I said finally.

"You know about the magic weapons that Vericat stole?" asked Todimpuss, in disbelief.

"Liar liar!" said the tabby. "I've seen this before. You'll be telling us you've got the very Balls of Woool next. You'd say anything to save your filthy neck."

"No." I said. "The weapons are here. In Mewpiter's name I swear it."

"Where?" said Todimpuss.

"Hidden on The Stroker," I gasped. "My ship. But you can't kill me. You need me to show you where they are."

Just then, a messenger crashed through the trees. "It's started chief," he said, "somehow they've got across the river. They swam it wearing full armour and got amongst our dogs."

"It begins!" cried Todimpuss.

So hungry for war was he that I dared to hope that he'd forget me, leap into the first chariot he saw and ride to his ruin. And he did. The trouble was, he'd forgotten that I was still tied to it. When his dogs leapt forward, there was a sudden jolt and the rope began to fly out behind the departing chariot.

"Untie me!" I pleaded. To my surprise the jailer started to loosen the knots. I expect the Kitons had a reward for those Womps and my jailer hoped to claim it. He uttered all manner of curses under his breath as he struggled to get the knots undone. "By the Mother's Pits – I've double knotted it!" was the last thing I heard before the rope sprung tight and I was dragged off screaming, on a ride that I will never forget.

ON THE ROAD

I will now say a word on the subject of roads. The road-builder's art is an ancient one. I picked up a lot of knowledge about roads from my dear friend Katrin back at Spatopia, where I used to live. Her second husband was a road builder from Purrsia and he swore that a straight road was a sign of a civilised country. He swore a lot, as I recall. At any rate, the ideal Roman road knows where it is going and is as smooth as a dinner plate. Kiton roads however, like to wander and wind between any points that might be of slight interest to the traveller. I swear that the road builders must be drunk as slaves at the Caturnalia festival (where three bowls of mead may be had for the price of one). As for the road surfaces, there are ruts and potholes, ditches and puddles. Weeds and thorny brambles grow in the verges at the sides of Kiton roads – not to mention the stones.

In fact, the stones deserve a mention. There are small stones thrown up by the chariot's wheels, that hit you in the eyes and big flints that knock lumps out of you when you land on them. On my short ride I became familiar with the terrors of life on the road, but as Fortune willed it, I live to tell the tale. I awoke in a daze, in the middle of what the Kitons call a 'gorse bush' – one of the worst plants in this land. The rope must have broken as I dangled from the back of the chariot. Mewlius himself mentioned that the Kitons are amongst the worst rope makers in the known world on account of their refusal to double wind their ropes.

Slowly, I crawled out to lick my wounds. I'd just started licking when the whiskers on my right side gave a sudden shudder. Looking up, I caught a glimpse of a figure by the tree line. I took it for a Kiton but it was dressed all in white.

"Mother of Mewpiter!" I cried. "This must be the Land Beyond." Although it looked very like the Land of the Kitons. It was still pouring with rain and I have never heard tell that there are gorse bushes on Mount Olympuss. Perhaps this was a forest spirit, or one of my ancestors? Without a word, the white shape turned and walked off into the forest. For some reason, and to this day I cannot tell you why, I sprung up and followed close behind.

WHITE SPIRIT

I crashed through the trees as I ran after the figure in white. I am not a fast runner and I feared that this was indeed a forest ghost. Perhaps it would lead me off a cliff, or into a crocodile nest? Every now and again I would see a flash of white ahead. And all the time that I was running, General Mawlus and Vespurrsian were attacking. Though I could see nothing but trees, I heard the shouts of battle. There was a great barking as the dogs of war were unleashed on both sides. Once they have been unleashed their handlers have a terrible job getting the wretched beasts back on their leashes again. Half of them run off after rats in the forest.

As well as the barking of the chariot dogs I heard battle cries, more like howls, in Kittish and also the occasional crash of heavy stones thrown from our slings. One of these whizzed past my ear and I lost my footing and tumbled headfirst into a muddy ditch.

To my surprise, I came face to face with a young figure with a fierce expression. She was a darker ginger than myself and her white robes could hardly be described as spotless. She seemed as surprised as I was by our meeting. For what seemed like an age, she said nothing. Uncomfortable with the long silence I started to make conversation,

"Looks like it's all started then. Sorry about the flying stones. Your lot are taking a hell of a beating, by the sound of it."

The stranger turned her head to one side.

"I probably shouldn't be saying this," I said, "but the Romans are used to fighting big hoards like yours. The bigger the hoard, the happier they are. Just look at what they did to the Purrmanians and the Mauls. It's not about personal bravery you see. It's about five thousand stabbing blades and scratching claws, working like one great animal."

"One big dumb animal," growled the stranger. "Now that you Catre are with the snail-eaters!" She spoke Catin with a thick accent.

In Peus's name, I thought, why does everyone keep calling me a Catre?

"I don't know what you mean about snail-eaters," I replied, "and I'm not a Catre. I'm not with any of your clans. So if you want to fight me, forget it."

"Fight you?" growled the stranger. "Do I look like I'm going to fight you?"

"Sorry," I began, "but the thought had crossed my mind." "I was told the females around these parts are more warlike than the males."

She was only young but often the young have the

quickest tempers. She certainly had a fierce look to her when she bristled.

"I'm a Mewid," she said in annoyance. "We don't do fighting. Surely you've heard of the Mewidic Code? It's used all over this land," she asked.

"A Mewid?" I replied, padding slowly backwards and sniffing the air for the smell of burning. "Sorry but I've always felt uncomfortable around sacrifices."

"Sacrifices are for the Higher Orders, I'm still a pupil. We only get to do curses, songs, poems and magic. My name's Furg."

"I'm Spartapuss." I replied.

"That barking is getting nearer," said Furg. "Time to leave."

Soon we were in the thick of the forest, heading down tracks and sidetracks that must have been left by creatures far smaller than ourselves. Often we would take what I thought to be the main path only to find ourselves on a side track. Furg seemed quite content with our progress but I had the feeling that we were winding around in circles.

"Are you sure you know where you're going?" I asked finally. "Only it's getting dark and I don't want to meet any night creatures. I hear that the crocodiles in this land have three eyes on their heads and hunt by night."

"I know exactly where we're going," laughed Furg.

"I'm sure we've been here before. I recognise that

burnt stump," I answered.

"There are plenty of those in the forest," she growled. "Our grove is near, there's only three oaks and hundred tails or so to go."

"Three oaks?" I said in surprise. "Have you been counting?"

"Yes," said Furg. "Well – sort of. To be honest I haven't passed woodcraft yet. I kind of lose concentration a bit. But I've got a great sense of smell, so I can always find anything in the end."

The darkness was gathering and it grew chill as we padded on through the forest. But the trees grew thicker and a gloomy mist rose from the forest floor that made it easy to lose your footing on a twisted root.

"Perhaps we ought to stop and wait for the moon to rise?" I suggested. "Do they teach you fire-making in woodcraft?"

"Wait here," said Furg, dashing towards a line of oaks.

I waited for a moment. But I could think of nothing but night creatures. So I rose quietly and followed her. Suddenly, the trees disappeared. It was not the edge of the woodland, just a treeless hole in the heart of the forest. It was good to see clear sky and stars above me, although the stars were strange compared to the ones in Rome. A full moon was rising. I wondered about the battle, Captain Kat, Tefnut and all my friends back in Rome. All of us looking at the same moon. These were my thoughts when I heard the blast of a great horn – like a trumpet, but deeper and somehow sadder.

I looked around quickly but there was no sign of Furg. The trees all around this gloomy glade were lined by shapes - figures all dressed in white.

"Who has come to our grove as the Hunter's moon rises?" said an ancient voice. It didn't sound like a proper question that needed an answer. And it wasn't exactly friendly. As the white figures moved in from the gloom, I caught their eyes, yellow as fangs. They let out a horrible howl.

> *Who comes – by the Hunter's moon?*
> *Who comes – to the grove of gloom?*
> *Who comes – from the ancient's tombs?*
> *Who comes – for the cutting?*

Mewlius Caesar was right! I thought. If this is singing, then it is the very least musical kind of singing that I had ever heard. It's tuneless droning, worse than the Purrmanians. Then I caught the glint of silver underneath white. Something sharp was hidden under their long robes.

"Who comes to The Cutting?" demanded the ancient voice.

"I am Spartapuss," I said, "and I can see that you've got a lot of cutting and singing and things to do, so I'd better leave you all to it."

Then I started to run, as fast as Purrcury, the god's

messenger, on a same day delivery. I got as far as a line of great oaks at the back of the grove when I saw them. More white figures padding noiselessly through the gloom. I sought shelter in the first tree, pressing myself flat against the trunk and searching for a hollow crack to hide in. But the Great Hunter would not let me hide, for his moon waxed high in the sky and lit the whole grove with its pale light. The light caught the yellow eyes of those unhappy creatures as they searched for me.

"Great goddess Fortune!" I said quietly. "It is time for another of our talks. I know I have called you a fickle old stray in the past. But help me now. Let this tree be hollow." But it was no use. My oak was young and strong, with no hollows to hide in. As the white figures advanced I had to do something. I made a desperate attempt to climb the first of the oaks, but I am no climber. In my panic I lost my grip and came crashing to the forest floor. I rolled over and tried to claw the leaves from my eyes. Then I heard that dreaded horn blasting again and there was another great tuneless howl. A sea of white figures packed the grove and I saw that each of them carried a silver blade, curved like a sickle.

Now when I was young like Furg, I took a lot of care over my appearance and was known for my wardrobe. I once won third best-groomed slave at the Supreme Imperial Show. Clawdius, our Emperor, who was then my master, spent my prize money on a new scratching post. But these days I have no time for fashion. The last time I smartened myself up, by wearing a golden coin on my collar, it led to an age of trouble. But of all the outrageous outfits, the one I found myself wearing that night in the grove must take first prize. For atop my head was a twist of oak leaves, wet and half-rotting, all bound up with a creeping green tree plant with white berries, known in this land as mistletoe. Seeing this tangle of leaves on my head, the Arch-Mewid shouted "Wait Mewids! Look! He wears the Oak Crown."

And with that every Mewid stepped back and lowered his silver sickle.

I was a little worried when the blindfold came out. But I must confess that after all that walking it was nice to be carried back here to the camp on a litter. The Secret Way is no better than any other road in this damp land and I got quite a shaking. But that is better than being skinned with a silver sickle. It was nice of them to let Furg travel with me. The refreshments weren't up to much. I didn't care for the dish that the Mewids call Spotted Dog – I was wondering what the spots were made of. My head was stuffed like a dormouse – full of questions. Furg did her best to answer them.

"I don't understand" I began in a rage. "First they were trying to hook me to death and now they are plumping up my cushions and feeding me treats."

"I told you to wait," said Furg.

"But you just ran off and left me in the dark, in the middle of the forest. Why didn't you say something?" I demanded.

"I was excited when I got a scent of my clan. Next time you'd better stay put like you're told," she laughed.

"What in the name of Mewpiter were they doing with those hooks?" I asked.

"Cutting the toes off the mistle," said Furg. "I forgot it was a ceremonial night in the Mewid calendar, or I would never have taken you there. I skipped that class because we'd spotted this fat rabbit near our dorm.

"I see," I replied. I could see by her eyes that she was telling the truth.

"Look on the bright side. Now you are crowned Oak King you are to become an honoured Mewid of our Order."

"Thank you," I replied, without much enthusiasm. "I must confess I have never liked ceremony. I have a terrible memory for rituals. I only go to the temple if I'm ordered to.

"What were they doing with those silver hooks?" I asked. Furg explained that the Mewids honour two plants above all others. The oak and the mistletoe. The two are always together and they grow the mistletoe in special groves of oak trees. It is harvested three times a year by means of silver sickles. This age-old ceremony is called The Cutting. Now Mewlius Caesar mentions a similar ritual in his book, but it ends in... I shall not say what it ends in. At any rate, according to Furg, old Mewlius seems to have got the wrong end of the sickle. The Mewids he saw in the woods were simply collecting white berries for a ceremony. I thought for a moment, before asking:

"Is there anything else I need to know, about The Cutting?"

"Nope," replied Furg, scratching her ear and adding, "It's a very ancient and important ceremony."

"I won't be expected to sing or act or anything, will I?" I asked. "Only I'm terrible at learning lines."

"Don't worry Oak," she replied. "You'll be fine." Her tail flicked and she picked at her teeth with a thin claw.

"Furg," I said, "You haven't got a clue about this ceremony have you?"

"Of course I have," she said.

I gave her a searching look.

"No idea," she finally admitted. "All I know is that they said that you are The Oak King, and I have to stay with you. That makes me something called The Keeper of the Oak and I get double points towards the ritual part of my Bardic exam. So you see, it is a very important ceremony for me."

As we entered the Mewid camp there was great excitement. Fires blazed everywhere. I was mobbed by young Mewids excited to see a stranger. That night many songs were sung till the fires burned low and the cries of forest creatures pierced the night's silence. I must admit, I was less disturbed by these cries than by the Kiton's tuneless singing. Still, it was nice to have all these fellows leaping about in my honour.

I could not help but think of Mewlius Caesar's words about the Mewid religion. "A savage infection that spreads across the world. The only cure is the sword." I had been ready to believe it before, but clearly there were two sides to the Mewids. The horror of the grove and now this song and dance side.

A large, good-humoured crowd had gathered around us.

"Say something," said Furg.

"What should I say?" I asked.

"I dunno," shrugged Furg.

"You're supposed to be the Keeper of the Oak. Help me out," I whispered in a half hiss.

"Why don't you just make something up?" she asked.

A young Mewid leapt over a bonfire, narrowly avoiding getting a singed tail on the way down.

"Well done!" I called lamely.

"Tell them that The Oak King salutes them!" said Furg. I did as my Keeper said, only to find that one of the leapers gave me a gesture that I shall not now record. Then he turned his back on me and pulled his tail between his legs.

"Ignore him," laughed Furg. "They're nothing to

do with us. They must be practising fire-leaping for Sam-mane."

"What's that?" I asked.

"A big festival," grunted Furg, "for the Ancestors."

Before I could ask, she continued. "I, er missed that lesson when Purn and me saw the Cawracle fly over the camp. We tried to track him through the forest to his nest – it's full of golden feathers they say - but we lost him. Found this big trout mind you. It was sweet when we roasted it. Don't tell anyone."

There was something bitter and sad in her, as if the good times she described would never come again. I had the feeling that Furg had missed lots of lessons like this. Although she was no scholar she was a proud Mewid, and was keen that I should join her in the Order. Although I was not convinced, Furg spent some time listing what she called 'The Rewards'."

"Look on the side that's bright, as we say round here," she said. "Being a Mewid is not all singing and fun. But at the end there's proper rewards to be had. We can visit any clan in the land and they have to offer us a basket for the night and their best food for as long as we choose to stay."

"I bet they love it when you lot turn up," I laughed. "And if their finest food is anything like the spotted dog, I think I'd rather hunt for myself."

"And there's the fighting," said Furg.

"Fighting?" I said. "I thought you said you didn't do fighting?"

"Exactly," said Furg. "We can't! It's forbidden by the code. The old ones always say that The Mewids is one of the safest professions you can get. It's a great job for your kittens as there's no danger of them getting killed in a clan war."

"Are there wars where you come from?" asked Furg with a flick of the tail.

I nodded. Although part of me longed to tell her of my home, I held back. So I poked at the dying fire with a bent stick and kept silent.

BACK TO SCHOOL

The youngest Mewids are fascinated to watch me writing. They can sit for hours at a time, their eyes glued to me as if the strangest magic could explode from my pen at any time – which is not very likely. They can sit for longer than my paw can stand to write. So I will turn in for the night now and pick up my diary in the morning. It is sure to be an interesting episode – I am told that I am to sit in on lessons tomorrow and Furg is to be my partner for studies.

MEWNONIUS XI

(June 11th)

NOT A GOOD FIRST day at school. Wanting to make a good impression, I asked Furg if I could borrow her notes.

"We have no notes here. We work from memory," she reminded me. So I asked if she could explain a little of the history of the Ancient Bards, who are the Mewid's singers and poets.

When they heard this, the others began to circle around Furg, reciting verses very quickly. The leader in this was an irritating youngster named Ruff. Furg told them to stop and gave Ruff a good knock on the ear. It was not claws-out stuff but Furg was embarrassed – whether on my part or for her own sake, I cannot say. As we left the class, Ruff and the others were rolling around laughing. I am not looking forward to lessons tomorrow.

MEWNONIUS XII

(June 12th)

LESSONS DID NOT go well as I struggle with Old Kittish – the tongue which most of the Mewids' stories are sung in. We were told to learn a part of the Ballad of Curious Thomas. Having learned the original, we were to compose our own verses to tell the story – in rhyme. It is a three-year song cycle that teaches Young Thomas to live in a state of right word, right thought and right deed. By the end of it, I was in a right state. The idea of being nice and not saying or thinking anything bad about others is very much to be admired. However,

I was not doing that well for I had already broken all three rules. I used the wrong word for 'chicken' in my poem, causing the class to break out into howls of laughter. Ruff was smirking at my mistake so Furg aimed a sly swipe at him as he got up to read his verse. As for right thoughts - I could only think that I would gnaw off one of my own limbs to escape that dreary droning.

"By Woool's Balls, that was dull," said Furg.

"Are lessons like this every day?" I asked, no longer so sure that I was cut out for the life of a Mewid.

"Worse sometimes," she replied. "That Curious Thomas is a sad case. He stole the King's cream so why not just eat it and have done with it? Why carry it around where everyone can see it? He must have fluff for brains."

Furg swung a paw at a passing butterfly and missed. I could tell that she was no more of a scholar than I am myself.

"Does every Mewid need to learn that stuff?" I said. "What about those I saw in the Grove? They didn't look like poets."

"They are the Kream," she replied. "They don't have to pass their Bardic exams."

"Why don't you try that?" I asked.

"They have to take a test, instead," she sniffed. "Only two in five get through it."

"Only two in every five pass?" I said. "That doesn't sound like good odds."

"The Kream always rise to the top, it is said."

"Still, you've got nothing to lose by trying," he replied.

Furg shook her head. "No thanks. I'm not ready for Summerlands yet." She lowered her eyes and gazed into the forest.

"Summerlands?" I asked.

"The other world, where the ancestors wait for us. It's like here only hotter. And it only rains once a month. That's where... " She was about to tell me something but she stopped short.

"Furg, my friend," I said. "Listen to me. If you hate this place so much, why not just leave it behind?"

She shook his head sadly. "I have wished for that so many times but there is my family to think about." Although her mother died when she was young, she was taken in by her aunt, a Micini of high pedigree.

"How much can your family mind if it is making you so unhappy?" I asked.

"Those who leave are known as The Cursed Ones. They are shunned by all the clans," she said.

"That doesn't sound very like "right word, right deed, right thought" to me," I answered.

"We were born to our paths," said Furg, "and I must follow mine as the crow flies." "Besides," she added, "my aunt would kill me.'

MEWNONIUS XIII

(June 13th)

OUR STUDIES WERE interrupted today. We had no
time to finish the Ballad of Curious Thomas. It
was a day of wrong words, wrong deeds and wrong
thoughts. The sound of a horn stopped Furg in the
middle of her verse and the whole class sprung up and
ran to the window. Outside a Mewid in torn robes had
arrived. In ten minutes his news was all around the
camp. Rome had won the battle of the river, scattering
the Kiton armies into the trackless marshes. Nothing
now stood between the Romans and the great city
of Camulod. Sitting on a heap of trophies, General
Mawlus had read out an order from the Emperor
himself. It was a death sentence for the Mewids. It
included not only members of the order but their
families and anyone found sheltering them. Furg said
it was no idle boast, for the General had already sent
soldiers into the woods and marshes. Standing stones
were being smashed and trees were being felled and
burned. The fear was that the Romans would go deep
into the forests to find the Mewids' sacred groves and
lay waste to them.

"Have no fear!" I said to Furg. "The Romans
couldn't find a sacred grove even if you gave them
a mistletoe map. They'll probably just chop down a
few trees and get lost. They'll be lucky to get back to

barracks before dinner."

But it was more serious than that. That night there were whispers around the camp that some Romans had come across a group of Mewids in the woods, as they were collecting mistletoe. There were no survivors. There was another rumour that the Arch-Mewid was holding back the truth in order to prevent a panic.

"Death take the Romans and all their kind," hissed Furg. She hadn't touched her dinner. Suddenly she went quiet as the grave. Then she sprung under the table – fast as a sling bullet. She emerged holding a tiny black mouse in one claw.

"What right have they to do this to us?"

"Only the right of the strong over the weak," I said.

"They are a race of butchers," spat Furg, letting the mouse go. "Led by a half-brained manic. They'll destroy us all."

"Clawdius has many faults," I said. "He is greedy, mean and jealous, but he is not mad. He's far smarter than he looks."

"That will be of great comfort when he burns us alive and lays waste to our cities," said Furg.

I shook my head. "That is not the Roman way," I explained. "Clawdius is far more likely to bribe a few local kings, collect a lot of taxes and get the first ship home."

"He's a crazy killer," said Furg. "It is said that he drinks the blood of the young, to cure his sickness. All the Caesars are cursed with the sickness."

"Where did you hear that?" I asked.

"Every Kiton knows it. It is taught in school," she replied with a flick of the tail.

"Well it's not true," I said.

"How do you know?" snapped Furg. She played with her chicken, stalking it around the bowl.

"The Romans have wronged you," I said. "But that does not make them all monsters. You are wrong about Clawdius, at any rate."

"What do you know of it?" snapped Furg.

And then I heard myself saying. "Who could know better than I? For I served Clawdius for most of my life."

"What?" growled Furg, spinning round to meet my eyes.

"I was his slave," I said.

"In Rome?" gasped Furg. I thought she was going to choke with rage.

"Yes," I admitted.

"No wonder you defend him, turntail. Perhaps you serve him still!" spat Furg. I thought she was going to strike me, but instead she backed off, growling.

"A Roman?" she spat. "By the Great Mother, I have taken up with a Roman liar." And she stalked off before I could explain.

There was nothing to be done. So I took my old friend Tefnut's advice and decided to do nothing. I made my way back to my sleeping place and I was thinking about whether to venture out for some water when I heard noises outside. An angry crowd of young Mewids had gathered outside. News had obviously travelled fast for there was graffiti all over the hut – showing in pictures what they do to turntails in these parts. My basket had been torn to pieces. I was wondering about how best to leave, when there was a voice at the door. Three tall Mewids, Kream by the look of them, had arrived to escort me away for my own safety.

Now I must go for I hear noises outside and I fear this diary may be discovered.

MEWNONIUS XIV

(June 14th)

Put to the Test

I write this, not knowing who will read it, or what will become of me.

I am told that the Mewids record the names of those who do not survive their test in epic ballads. I am pleased to hear that these poems are not sung, but rather told alongside a winter fire, usually at the end of the evening when everyone else has run out of more popular material. The Arch-Mewid's assistant, the Head Bard, was very polite and asked what name

I'd like to be known by in the tales, in the event that I fail to survive. Now I have always loved the tales of the great figures of the past who have names that call down the centuries and tell us of their character. What would they call me? I decided on Spartapuss the Loose Tongued. But Spartapuss the Blabber Mouth or Spartapuss Fence Sitter might have been better.

The two tall Mewids who were my escorts led me outside. Each Mewid carried a silver sickle, like the ones I had seen in the grove.

"Where are we going?" I asked, knowing that I had little choice.

"The Arch-Mewid has called you to a meeting at his High Seat," said the first. He said this as if a meeting at the 'High Seat' had some importance.

Soon we were winding our way through a dense forest on tracks that climbed steadily upwards. Unexpectedly, we reached the shores of a dark lake. The water was black and although I was thirsty, I did not dare to slake my thirst, as the Kitons would say. On the far shore was a steep slope, completely bare save for a few lightning trees that were clinging on stubbornly. Stones covered the slope. From a distance they looked small, like fine grey sand, but when we got up close I saw that some of them were great boulders, as big as chariots. It was a steep climb on a path that seemed at times well-trodden and at times little more than a rabbit track. The lake disappeared behind us as we climbed. Then I saw the stone circle. It was as if the hillside had a mouth and here were its teeth – gnarled and jagged, standing black against a blanket of grass. The whiskers on my right side would not stop twitching. I had to scratch at them to get them under control.

"Hail!" said an ancient voice. It was the same cracked voice I had heard that night in the grove.

"Hello?" I whispered in reply.

A flat-eared cat appeared from behind the sun and leapt up onto the tall altar stone. He looked older than the ancient stones. His silver knife glittered in the morning sun. Now I was in the middle of the circle. There was a rasping blast on a tuneless trumpet and in a heartbeat, a host of Mewids appeared from behind the stones. There was a terrible howling from one of them. They advanced towards me. For a moment I thought of the dreadful tales recorded by Mewlius Caesar, about Mewids and their strange rituals.

"Do not fear us!" said the cracked voice.

"Do I look afraid?" I replied.

"Yes," said the Arch-Mewid, for it was he.

"Well perhaps I'd enjoy my visit more if everyone I met wasn't armed to the teeth."

"We are at war, Spartapuss, in case you hadn't noticed," said the cracked voice.

"Why have you brought me here?" I asked.

"Surely you know why," said the Arch-Mewid. There was no way out. I was surrounded by armed

Mewids – Kream at that. The grey stones of the circle looked like they could hold me inside forever.

"Am I here for a... " My words trailed away. I could not say the word 'sacrifice'. Deep inside, I feared that if I said it, it would come true – sure as the rain on the rocks.

"Have no fear," said the Arch-Mewid, "our young are headstrong but they will obey their elders. That is the way of the Mewid. As for your study partner," he added, "well you have my apologies. She will cause you no more trouble." A flick of the tail betrayed his anger.

Poor Furg, I thought. But if she didn't have the guts to leave this bizarre order, then that was her problem.

"Seldom do we let outsiders into this circle," said the Arch-Mewid. "But today you are not our only guest."

There was another loud blast on the horn.

A ragged cat stalked towards the altar stone. He was covered in dirt, with a matted coat. The Arch-Mewid gave him a searching look.

"Enter friend. But remember where you are," he said.

"Peace sit with all within these stones," growled the stranger.

I looked at the Arch-Mewid. What was this place? A temple or a court?

"Now you may question our friend the Oak here,"

replied the Arch-Mewid with a flick of the tail. My new interrogator stalked towards me.

"You," began the stranger with a hiss. "You were the last person to see my brother alive."

And then I realised that this dirty creature, in all his rags was Caractapuss, Prince of the Kitons. When we last met he had been groomed and well spoken. His easy charm was another casualty of war.

"You would do well to tell me everything you know," he spat. I felt the eyes of the Mewids on me. Then I heard myself saying:

"Your brother had many questions too, I'll tell you what I told him."

"I am not so easily deceived," spat Carac and he sprung towards me.

"Enough," said the Arch-Mewid. "You must respect the laws of this circle or go."

"Go?" hissed Carac. "Perhaps I should take my army and go. But who will save the Mewids then? Already the Romans are hunting for your groves. When you taste oak smoke on the morning wind, remember my words."

From around the circle there were howls, followed by shouts of approval.

"Guests are safe within these stones," said the Arch-Mewid. "Spartapuss, you are free to speak or not, as you please."

"There is little to tell," I went on. "Todimpuss took me for questioning. He was asking questions when your messenger arrived saying that the Romans were attacking. Then he took off."

Carac looked me in the eyes. "What lies did you tell him to make him disappear like that? Why didn't he join me on the battlefield?"

"I have no clue," I replied.

"Liar!" hissed Carac again.

"Alright," I said. "You press me so I will give you it all on a plate. Your dear brother tried to kill me. He had me tied between two chariots, whilst he was asking his questions. And he rode off with me still tied to his. By rights, I should have been dragged to pieces. But the rope snapped or the knot gave way."

Carac moved low to the ground and turned sad circles, shaking his head.

"It is said that you cannot find a master rope maker in this land, and I thank Fortune that it has proved to be," I said.

"The fool!" growled Carac. "And I am a fool too, now my word is broken. For I swore an oath to our father that I would protect him."

I felt a chill. Perhaps it was the wind as it raced between the ancient stones. All of a sudden I pitied this broken Prince of the Kitons.

"Listen," I said, "I think it was an accident. I don't think he was trying to kill me – he probably just wanted to scare me. Perhaps he just got excited when the messenger arrived and forgot to untie me before he drove off. And he lives still, as far as I know."

The Arch-Mewid looked me in the eyes.

"Spartapuss, a question, if I may. What was it that Todimpuss wanted to know?"

"He asked about Clawdius and the Romans," I replied. I thought about the Weapons of Magical Power. A part of me wanted to tell all to the Arch-Mewid, but instead I just stood still in the middle of those cold stones and held my tongue.

Then the caw of a crow broke the silence. I saw that it had landed on the tallest stone. There was a gasp from all present.

"The Cawracle! The Cawracle!" cried the Mewids.

As I looked around the circle, I saw that all there, including Carac, were avoiding the crow's gaze. But I have always had a fondness for crows. Good old Russell was one of my best friends back in my Spatopia days. But this grizzled old master was far bigger than Russell. And though he was old he was obviously a superior flyer, for he had made a perfect landing, without a sound, on the Altar Stone.

"What news from afar my friend?" I asked.

The Cawracle caught my gaze for a moment. He turned his great head to one side.

"Stop! I'll tell you about the Womps," said the Cawracle, in a voice exactly the same as my own. I stared at the bird in disbelief. Every Mewid save their leader was now face down on the muddy ground covering their ears.

Only Carac dared to speak. "Womps?" he asked softly.

"The magical weapons. The ones you asked for in your letter to Clawdius," said the Cawracle in perfect mimicry of my own speech. "Someone stole them."

I must confess that I hated the sound of my own voice. Surely my voice is not that squeaky, I thought to myself.

"Weapons?' asked Carac. He certainly seemed to know how to lead the crow in the right direction. I wondered if he had seen this before or heard about it in a song cycle.

"The weapons are here. In Mewpiter's name I swear it," squeaked the bird in a very high voice. I must have been in fear of my life when Todimpuss had questioned me.

I knew what was coming next.

"Where?" asked Carac.

"Hidden on The Stroker," gasped the Cawracle in mimicry of me choking. "My ship. But you can't kill me. You need me to show you where they are."

Then he flapped up to the alter stone.

"You can't kill me!" he said. And with that he was gone.

Without another word, Carac sprung out of the circle and took off after the bird.

So now the Mewids knew that I was a Roman, the name of my ship and about the Womps. Carac, desperate for news of his brother, knew about them too. It is a strange feeling to have all the things you have said brought out into the open. No wonder the Mewids had covered their ears. Perhaps that is the reason behind one of their great threes – "Right word." With birds like that flying around, it pays to think before you open your mouth.

I learned that the Mewids have sent spies to look over Carac. Many have tried to catch the Cawracle but all have failed, for none can run as the crow flies.

ANOTHER AUDIENCE

The next morning I was called to another audience with the Arch-Mewid. He had sat up through the long night, deciding what to do with me.

"It has been decided," he announced, "that you must take the test."

I could tell that this was not an invitation. And here the old Mewid gave me another of his long looks.

"It is for your own safety. Once you are a member of our order, you can live here with us."

"Let me go," I said. "I am weary of this land. Let me slip away and I'll never to speak a word of what I have seen."

The old Mewid shook his head.

"Impossible!" he replied. "After what happened in the circle, the order could never allow such a risk."

I did not care to ask what would happen if I refused to take this test. At least it was to be quick. I remained inside the hut until lunchtime whilst the preparations were being made. Rain fell in sheets blown on the wind. When the Mewids appeared outside the door, I knew that they had come to take me to the test. Again we made the long walk through the forest, and rain fell like spears on a battlefield. Even the weather was wild in this land.

I had no clue what to expect of the Mewids' test. I have always had a horror of examinations. I should not think that notes would be allowed in this one.

As we reached the near shore of the black lake, my eyes stood out on stalks. There, before me stood a monstrous cat – over thirty tails high. The sight of it made me feel quite ill. It was, of course, one of the Kiton's celebrated wicker statues. If you ask me, wicker is not a suitable material for statues. Wicker for baskets and hovels – yes. Wicker for monstrous statues – in Peus' name, no thank you! I have never been fond of statues. And this one, made entirely out of straw and cane, was way behind the artistry of our Roman statues. My thoughts were interrupted by a solemn blast on the horn again. "Ha!" I said to myself, for I had thought to myself this very morning, that whatever this test is about, I bet they use that horn to start it.

The Arch-Mewid approached and I made myself ready.

"So, you are ready," he said with a touch of gloom in his cracked voice.

Before I could answer, my mind was made up for me.

"He is ready! He is ready!" cried the Mewids behind me.

The whiskers on my right side gave a twitch. They led me underneath the feet of the great wicker cat and up a thin beam. As I climbed towards to the middle of the statue, there was an unusual smell in the air. Now I had a plain view into the heart of the statue – and I made out another narrow ladder leading upwards into a cage.

"You will stay here for the night," said the Arch-Mewid. "And when we meet again in the morning, be ready to tell me what you dreamed."

"Is that it?" I said.

"That is all," said the Arch-Mewid. When I climbed the final ladder, they pulled the door of the cage shut and the ladder was withdrawn. I sat on a tiny ledge, fifty tails or more above the ground. As my eyes grew accustomed to the gloom I saw that the belly of the statue was full of ladders.

It is a pity there's no ladder down, I thought to myself.

So here I sit, waiting for sleep to come to me, for I cannot come to it. Perhaps it is the chill night air. Also, the basketwork on the floor is of a very poor quality and I have to take care not to spike myself. There is nothing to do but fall asleep and dream, and remember what I have dreamed. Then tell it all to the Arch-Mewid tomorrow if, Fortune willing, I will come through this.

MEWNONIUS XXX

(June 30th)

School's Out

Again I take up my diary. And when I roll back to my last entry I find there is so much to tell that I will not have the time to get it all down in one sitting.

I shall pick up the tale when I was trying to sleep. I cannot say whether or not I was asleep when I heard a voice calling:

"Wake up Roman,"

At last! I thought, a dream! I shall have a dream for the Arch-Mewid. There was something familiar about that voice.

"Roman!" called the voice. "Awake!"

I thought what kind of dream is that, to be woken by a familiar voice that you cannot place? I shall have to do better than that for the Arch-Mewid.

Then something hit me hard on the nose.

"Aaaagh!" I cried.

"Stop whining and wake up!" hissed the voice.

I peeped through a gap in the wicker and saw Furg fitting another stone into her sling.

"I should have guessed as much," I said. "What in Peus's name do you want?"

"Get your fat rump down here," she said nervously glancing behind her.

"Go away," I replied. "I am in the middle of a test. How am I supposed to dream something for the Arch-Mewid with you prowling around all night?"

"I'm here to do you a favour," she said sulkily. "What do you think will happen tomorrow if the Arch-Mewid doesn't like what you tell him?"

"I have no clue," I replied. "I expect I'll fail the test."

"You'll be toast," she said matter-of-factly.

"Whatever do you mean by that?" I asked, now not so sure that I wanted to hear it.

"The tests always end in flames. Look over there, if you don't believe me. It seems they're not too hopeful about your results."

From the other side of the wicker cat's tail, I saw a red glow. A thin column of smoke was rising.

"Looks like they've got the fire going already," said Furg.

It did not take long for me to make up my mind. I made my way back down to the belly and was clawing at the ladder, with a view to using it to climb down from the statue. But it was too short! As Fortune willed it, Furg got hold of a longer ladder, which had been tucked away out of sight behind one of the paws of the great statue. With care, I made my way down. Before long we were creeping away down the track, away from the black lake and that dreadful grinning statue.

"Thank you Furg my friend... " I began.

"You're no friend of mine, Roman," she replied. After a meaningful pause she added, "I came back for a reason."

"Really?" I replied. "And what reason might that be?"

"You will take me to the ship – to the Weapons of Magical Power. I am going to steal them back."

"I see," I said, "and what will you do with them?"

"None of your business, turntail," she hissed.

"Bring them back to the Arch-Mewid, so he'll let you back in? I've got a feeling that's not going to work."

"I will take them to Carac," she hissed, so he can bring fire on you and your turntail friends."

And right there and then, a thought came to me. I could stand the endless rain and the tasteless food, but I had had a bellyfull of the Land of the Kitons. There was worse prejudice against me here, amongst my own kind, than I had ever known back in Rome. Even the Mewids, who I had started to respect, were about to set me on fire. I decided that the Kitons could fight their own battles. And as for Clawdius – I had him to thank for sending me to this charmless place. I would make my escape by the first ship. My destination – any place but here.

"So, it is settled. You will lead me to the Womps?" asked Furg, who seemed slightly annoyed that I'd agreed to her plan so readily.

"Gladly,' I laughed, "but there is one problem. Where in Peus's name are we?"

ON THE TRACKLESS MARSHES

Three days and nights have passed since Furg came to rescue me from that statue. And ever since the rain has got harder and colder. Furg is no warmer either. She avoids my gaze and will not speak except about the task ahead of us. She is sure we are on the right track for the river, which will take us to the coast. There we will try to find the ship. I hope for my sake that the Womps are still on it when we get there.

I have given some thought as to how to get away from this land. I will find a hiding place on a passing ship or sneak aboard as one of the crew. As a cook perhaps? Reasonable cooks must be in short supply in this part of the world.

CATILIS VII

July 7th

I Begin Again

HERE I BEGIN my new diary, as the old one is lost. My time here has been utterly pointless. I have been of no use to either side. I was beginning to think that I could serve some purpose by keeping an account of the events for the sake of history. But now that my diary is under a marsh, I have failed in that too. I will perhaps rewrite some of it from memory if I get the chance.

It is days since I last took up my pen, and Fortune has been spinning again. There are so many threads now that my clumsy paw cannot unpick the truth of them. I am like a young bird fallen from the nest which flaps around in circles, unable to get off the ground. But I suppose that I must count myself lucky to have avoided the many unhappy foxes that prowl this damp and unforgiving land. But by good chance, here I am on a mat in a Roman tent once again.

I will take up my story back in the trackless marshes.

They were not in fact entirely trackless, in the same way that the Blue Mountains are not entirely blue. In fact the tracks in these marshes are well known to the local Mewids, and to some oyster hunters and the

119

like. The Romans crossed and re-crossed these ancient paths without even noticing them – as a snail creeps through spilt beer - until Fortune drew them to us.

"What's that?" I whispered, turning towards Furg who was some way behind me. When I spun around she was gone. The next thing I heard was a howling hiss. Without a second thought, I sprung towards the spot where I thought the cry came from.

Three attackers had set upon Furg. She was fighting with tooth and claw but they were gradually getting the better of her.

"Halt! Halt!" I shouted.

"Halt?" exclaimed their leader, in surprise. He was lean and muscled, with a black face and cold eyes. Neither Furg nor the auxiliaries stopped fighting.

"Call them off!" was all I could think of to shout.

"Why?" laughed Black-face through bared teeth. He had a cold voice to go with his cold eyes.

There was something unusual about his accent, although his Catin was good. I thought for a moment and then replied.

"I am a Roman citizen. In the name of Emperor Clawdius, you'd better do what I say," was the best I could do. It was a lie of course, for I am a mere freed-cat, and not a citizen. My opponent looked me up and down and spat.

"A Roman?" he said, his head turned to one side in disbelief. He must have been thinking that with my colouring, I looked very like one of the locals.

"What about her? Is she a Roman too?" he said. The biggest cat, who had wide brown eyes, now had Furg pinned. His fighting partner, who had a torn ear, now padded back from the fray. He was a tawny colour, except for the white tip of his tail, which looked like it had been dipped in a bowl of cream.

"We have orders to kill the enemy," said Brown-eyes.

"Kill them dead," added White-tail, rather pointlessly.

"Let go of her immediately. She's a Mewid priestess," I said matter-of-factly. I am taking her to General Mawlus for questioning."

Furg let out a low hiss and gave me a murderous look that was very convincing.

"So you'd better stop mauling her or you'll be telling old Iron Claws how sorry you are."

It seemed that Fortune had spun me a good one, for these were Vespurrsian's soldiers – auxiliaries from the XIV Hisspanic. They knew little of General Mawlus except that he had a fierce reputation, and that he was their own commander's superior. At a signal from Black-face they let Furg go. She backed off – still spitting fury – to the cover of a mound of dead reeds, rotted by rain that never stops.

"If that's a Mewid priestess, then I'm the King of Tray!" spat Brown-eyes. He stared at Furg as he licked a claw that he'd torn during the struggle.

As my friend Cursus used to say, "When caught with a small lie, there's only one thing you can do - make it bigger."

"She's the Arch-Mewid, actually," I said.

The three let out a gasp.

"Dungheaps!" said Black-face, "She's no Arch-Mewid. She's too young."

"Of course she's young. Arch-Mewids aren't allowed to live past their fifth birthday - they go off if they don't get sacrificed.'

Black-face smiled and Brown-eyes gave a little gasp at the thought of this.

"Every Roman knows this. Doesn't Vespurrsian tell you auxiliaries anything?' I asked, shaking my head and trying to sound puffed up, like a proper citizen.

"This is not news to me," said Black-face. "In their groves, we found silver knives," he whispered. "Shaped like the crescent moon."

"Listen to my instructions," I said, trying not to sound as if I was thinking aloud. "You will escort us both to the coast immediately, where we will await the arrival of the General."

Brown-eyes said nothing. He was still looking at Furg. The rest of the party began to laugh.

"Time is short. We must leave now," I added.

The laughter grew louder and louder.

"You will have to escort yourselves," he hissed.

"Explain yourself," I demanded.

"We're lost," admitted White-tail.

There was a triumphant laugh from behind the rotten mound of reeds. Furg was playing her part convincingly but she had to be careful. Auxiliaries are the toughest troops in the army. They are sent in first, when the commander daren't risk Roman lives, or when there is dirty work to be done.

These three soldiers had been split up from the rest of their cohort, who had got a scent of some Mewids in the trees and decided to chase them without waiting for orders. Since then they had strayed through the unforgiving forest, turning circles until they were hopelessly lost. They had decided to go to low ground, where they might find a river and follow it. Then they came upon the marshes and tried to cross by means of a faint track, ringed by blue flowers. Black-face, whose real name was Hissero, was the highest ranking of the three. When they stumbled on the track he had commanded them to stop while he decided what to do. They followed the promising track but it had led to a stale pool, so they tried to retrace their steps. That had been four days ago and they had wandered since. Whichever way you looked, there were tangled reeds, tail high.

"Where were you going citizen?" demanded Hissero.

Now I had some explaining to do.

"This is a Mewid track," I explained, "she was leading the way."

"Come out here my pretty and tell your uncle

123

where to go," said Brown-eyes. I regret that Furg did just this. It's a good thing that her insults were in the Kitish tongue, or the auxiliaries would have skinned her on the spot.

"Don't overdo it or you'll get us both killed," I growled under my breath. Then I had a terrible thought. Perhaps Furg was not play-acting. Did she think that I planned to take her to General Mawlus? That I had betrayed her? By the way she was skulking that was certainly a possibility.

"Come out Mewid, or I'll drag you out," spat Hissero. But Furg had no intention of doing as she was told. She was working her way towards another a bank of rotten reeds, now just within springing distance.

"Get your prisoner under control, citizen" demanded Hissero.

"Do not be alarmed. She's always climbing around the place. She's probably got a scent of mistletoe."

"In the marshes?" growled Hissero.

"Don't ask me. It's part of their religion," I said.

Then, three things happened all at once. The whiskers on my right side gave a twinge, Furg sprung from her perch and bit Brown-eyes on the nose, and down the track came a Kiton battle chariot, at full tilt. The lead dogs were wild eyed – the right dog looked mad with fear. Hissero and White-tail leapt out of the way leaving me in the chariot's path.

BENEATH THE WHEELS

I have never had a lot of luck with chariots, as readers may remember. I have been dragged behind one, feeling the hurt of every stone. I have crashed one, in the Arena. But until this unhappy moment, I have never had the experience of being run down by one. As a kitten I had a horrible fear of wheels and wondered which would be worse – the thick wheel of a cart crushing the bones of your tail or the thin wheel of a chariot slicing it in two. These thoughts came to mind as I felt the hot breath of the lead dog in my face. I wondered if the dogs could bite you whilst they were running over you. Rather than staring death in the face, I closed my eyes. I heard the shout, but I did not see the dogs take a tiny step to the left. I was dragged up by the collar and into the hurtling chariot.

I did not have time to thank Furg or the driver before Fortune got behind her wheel again.

"Be still! In the name of Woool," boomed the driver.

Perhaps it was the extra weight or my movements, but the lead dog on the right side lost her footing. I had been pulled from under the wheels of a chariot only to crash in one.

I remember little of the accident, save the desperate search for Furg in the wreckage. We were both thrown clear but our driver was not so lucky. I stood above him as Furg loosened the straps on his helm and removed the eye-piece.

"Save it from our enemies," he gasped.

"What do you think he's talking about?" I asked Furg.

"Shut up Roman. It is not for you," spat Furg.

Todimpuss, the Prince of the Kitons, who had treated me so cruelly drew in his last breath. "See you in Summerlands," were the last words he spoke with it.

Not knowing what to do, I padded away from the scene.

It was a sorry scene but I could not cry false tears over him. In truth I was disappointed about Furg. I had been touched that she had thought to rescue me. But now she was as hostile as ever.

The chariot was hopelessly wrecked so I saw to it that the dogs were unleashed. Those of them that could run got away into the reeds. One was left howling over the broken body of its fallen partner. Chariot wheels and dog harnesses were strewn around, slowly sinking into the bubbling marsh.

Then, in the midst of all this I noticed something. It was already half-way under the mud. On the side I could make out some writing. First an A and then an R. The word ended in the letters US.

"Furg!" I called. "Look over here!"

Making my way from reed clump to reed clump I inched towards it and rubbed the side with my paw.

"Furg!" I called again. Still she refused to answer.

Leaning forward, I wiped at the dirty writing with

outstretched paw. After some wiping with marsh water, its message was revealed. It said "NARKITTUS".

"Furg! Get over here now!" I called. "I've found Narkittus's crate." There was no answer.

Cursus once told me that females are so hard to understand on account of their brains being put in upside down. Although I have never believed such nonsense, I must admit that I could not understand the way Furg thought.

"The crate!" I called. "It's got your Weapons of Magical Power in it. Remember? It's sinking into the marsh. You'll have to help me."

"We will help you citizen," said a cold voice behind me.

I thought about making some excuse but Hissero was no fool - they had Furg collared and gagged. The look that she gave me would have turned all the milk of Rome sour. Now she thought that our captors knew everything.

By the time we'd dragged the crate out, the light was fading. I expect that the Marsh Creatures were getting ready for their nightly hunts. Brown-eyes got a fire going by clever means of a flint and a small piece of metal. Where he found dry reeds, I have no clue. Soon, sparks and insects danced in the flickering flames. It might have been pleasant, if it was not for the rope on my collar. Hissero was taking no chances this time.

"Well, isn't this nice citizen?" said Hissero.

I made no reply.

"When are we going to open the box?" asked White-tail. "There's surely treasure in there."

"Nah. I heard him say it was weapons," said Brown-eyes.

"But what if there's golden shields or silver spears? Those sort of weapons."

White-tail padded lazily over to Furg and removed the gag.

"What's in the box, Mewid?" he said softly. But Furg did not answer.

Hissero gave me a questioning look. I avoided it for some time before saying:

"I have no clue what is in that box. Open it, if you must, for I cannot stop you."

White-tail walked up to the crate with greedy eyes.

"Go on then. Open it!" said Hissero. Furg let out a little hiss.

"Wait," said Brown-eyes, looking at Furg. "What if it's a trap? I wouldn't open it if I were you. Not if it's got anything to do with the Mewids. It could be cursed." White-tail backed away from the crate. Furg let out a little mew of disappointment.

"You," spat Hissero, "you will open it."

Furg sat motionless. No word passed her lips but every nerve and sinew in her body oozed with spite. I knew what was coming next.

"Obey me Mewid!" cried Hissero. He picked up a whip that White-tail had saved from the chariot wreck.

"Do as he says Furg," I pleaded. "There's no point getting yourself killed."

Hissero cracked the whip but Furg didn't move a muscle.

"Open the crate!" spat Hissero, cracking the whip at her again. "Open it now!"

"Wait!" I said. But Hissero wasn't going to wait. And Furg wasn't going to back down.

"Enough!" I cried. I sprung to the crate and began tearing at the lid, but it did not budge.

"For Peus's sake, it's nailed shut!" I gasped. "Has anyone got a lever?"

Brown-eyes handed me a tent peg, which I wedged into the seal and twisted. As the lid lifted, the crate gave out a great hiss and I leapt backwards in horror. Brown-eyes stopped shouting advice. White-tail stopped shouting at Furg. Hissero stopped cracking his whip. Then a familiar voice from behind me said: "That belongs to me."

How Narkittus had found us, I had no clue. It is the gossip at the Palace that he has eyes and ears everywhere and nothing can be said or done without him knowing about it. I must admit that I was almost pleased to see him. Hissero and the auxiliaries gave us no further trouble and surrendered the crate without argument. Whether it was Narkittus's superior manner or the century of armed guards behind him, that convinced them, I have no clue. But having a hundred soldiers behind you must add force to you words.

Narkittus has a way of speaking to the lower ranks as if they are very low indeed. Lower than worms in the ground, less than dirt. I would have thanked the Goddess that he said only six words to me when we met. Unfortunately, those words were: "You! You are coming with me."

At any rate, the crate was loaded onto a wagon without debate and we soon found ourselves on the march towards General Mawlus's camp. Mawlus, it seems, had rounded up his forces from the marshes, along with some of Vespurrsian's stragglers and established a makeshift HQ some fifty miles from the enemy capital of Camulod. When we reached camp, I was greeted with an armed escort that took me to Narkittus's tent. Inside it was grand, more like an apartment in the Palace than a soldier's tent. Furg however, was chained and led away. In a panic, I demanded to speak with Narkittus.

"He's busy,' said Narkittus's orderly, whose name was Grassus. He was a cheery old soul despite having only three legs, which were in constant use running around after Narkittus all day.

"His highness wants you to attend the briefing this afternoon," said Grassus. "And a word of advice: hold your tongue in front of General Mawlus. We have a saying in this legion, 'the nail that sticks up gets hammered down.'"

"Where have I heard that before?" I replied.

HEADS AND SPIKES

As I entered the briefing room, Vespurrsian was filing his claws with his long silver file.

"Put that down!" ordered General Mawlus. Vespurrsian put the file back into its case. "Intelligence?" growled the General wearily.

"Me?" asked Vespurrsian. "Sorry sir."

General Mawlus began to bristle. Vespurrsian reached for his notes.

"Our spies report that The Mewids won't be any bother. Seems they didn't put up much of a fight after all. Oh, and a bit of good news on the enemy Princes – we've just had reports that one of them is dead," began Vespurrsian.

"Which one?" demanded Narkittus.

"The stupid one," said Vespurrsian. "Prince To – Todo…"

"Todimpuss," growled Mawlus.

"Glad I won't be saying that again," said Vespurrsian under his breath.

"And the other prince has run off west. The rump of the Kiton army has gone with him. The rest of them fled after the battle. There is no sign of an army to defend Camulod. They say it's a capital city, but it wouldn't pass for a few hovels at home. Our spies report that the city walls are poorly constructed, "made of thin wood of a very poor quality," it says here."

"Your recommendation?" asked Mawlus.

"Well, I suppose we could bring some decent

Roman stone masons in and do a proper job of it."

"About the Kitons," sighed the General.

"Well, I should say we go after the enemy prince and when he's dead, we pop back, knock down the city walls and take the enemy capital," said Vespurrsian.

"Idiot!" said Mawlus. "Why do you think Prince Caractapuss has gone west? To draw us away from his city of course. No – we will take the city first and wait for him to return to the aid of his tribe. Then when he comes I will have his head on a spike, on the city walls for all to see."

"Excellent," said Vespurrsian.

"You'd better have him check with the stores to see that there are some spikes in stock," said Narkittus.

"Leave us," spat General Mawlus, "before I put your head on a spike!"

That's it for the Kitons, I thought to myself. Some of them were rude, others miserable, but I would not wish our legions on them. Although I had no love for Prince Caractapuss, I had no desire to see his head on a spike.

"General, aren't you forgetting something?" asked Narkittus.

"What might that be, Squeak?" said Mawlus.

"Your Emperor," replied Narkittus. "He is your commander in chief and according to the rules of war, he should have the honour of taking the enemy capital."

Mawlus stood very still.

"Now listen Narkittus," said Vespurrsian. "Nobody follows the rules of war anymore. They so old fashioned that they don't even teach them at the academy."

"Get out!" hissed Mawlus.

"Gladly," said Narkittus, motioning to me to follow, "but after I leave, I shall have to report to the Emperor that you ignored the rules of war. I'm afraid it could go very badly for you." Narkittus padded towards the door.

"This is ridiculous," cried Mawlus. "We have killed one enemy Prince. The other has fled. Their capital is at our mercy. If we call for Clawdius now it will be six weeks before he arrives. Six weeks before we can strike the winning blow."

"I think you'll find that technically, Todimpuss, being the elder brother, was a King. And killing a King can bring bad luck," said Narkittus.

"Nonsense!" growled the baffled Mawlus.

"According to the rules of war, killing an enemy King is the right of your commander in chief."

"What?" hissed Mawlus. "There's nothing in the rules about that." He glared at Narkittus, as if he was just about to stab him on the spot. Narkittus merely smiled.

"We'll let Clawdius be the judge of that, shall we? He loves judging. I saw him judge two thousand cases last year. The thing is that justice is not "blind" in his case. He gets so irritated. I saw him execute one

Sprisoner because it was nearly dinner time and there were mushrooms on the menu."

"This is… " interrupted Mawlus.

"And the one thing the Emperor cannot stand is interruptions," said Narkittus shaking his head slowly. "He cannot stand it when the defendants interrupt him saying that they are innocent."

THE ORDER

Before the sun had set, Mawlus sent a messenger to Rome with a letter asking for Clawdius's help. You can be sure that he used the correct wording, "Resistance is now so stiff that we need the Emperor, our commander in chief to win the day."

If Narkittus was pleased with himself for outflanking Rome's best General, he showed no sign of it. He sent me back to his quarters, escorted by a couple of scruffy looking guards. In all the confusion, I wondered if he had forgotten about Furg. General Mawlus's orders had come directly from the Emperor himself – all Mewids are to be executed.

I resolved to help her escape. I stalked over to the entrance of the tent. There was only old Grassus outside, keeping watch, but I didn't have the heart to fight my way past a three-legged veteran, so I stalked back to my basket in the corner and brooded. Poor Furg. Even if she escaped, could she go back to the Mewids, having run away from school?

Grassus came in about an hour later and tried to cheer me up with a 'wall fish' supper. The snails were nicely spiced. I thanked Paws, the God of Disagreements, that I had not decided to knock Grassus out. That night I went early to my basket and I was dreaming about burning oak trees, when I heard a noise. Narkittus sprung into the room. "Up up up!" he said, sounding unusually cheery. "There is much to be done. We only have six weeks to make the arrangements."

"Arrangements?" I replied, clambering out and padding over towards the snail plate for a second helping. "I am sure that General Mawlus will come up with a plan for glory for Clawdius. I have a healthy dislike of heads on spikes so I am thankful that he won't need my help to crush the Mewids."

"Crush the Mewids?" said Narkittus. "We are going to save the Mewids. Why in Peus's name do you think we were sent here?"

This revelation caught me mid-snail and I began to choke, sending the snail plate crashing to the ground.

"But – I don't understand," I spluttered. "I thought… "

"You thought I was a bullying bureaucrat. High-minded, with a hunger for power and a stone for a heart," said Narkittus.

"Er something like that," I replied.

"I am all those things. Perhaps that is why they have so much need of one like me."

"Who has need of you?" I gasped.

Narkittus laughed. He pulled from a bag at his collar something small and shiny. He held out a coin, just like the one Tefnut had given me long ago, at the Arena. The Fleagyptian gold was pale, but it shone very bright.

"I believe that you were once given a coin like this before," said Narkittus. "Your Fleagyptian friend told me to show you my coin as proof. Hard though it may be for you to believe, we both are both servants of same ancient Order."

"Tefnut told you that?" I asked in wonder. "But if the Order wants to help the Kitons, why can't they send them some proper help? What use are we?"

"This is a fight the Kitons could never win. Even if they stopped fighting amongst themselves. They are brave, but they don't have the tactics, organisation or equipment to defeat General Mawlus."

I heard myself saying, "And even if Mawlus was defeated, Clawdius would send another in his place."

"How wise you are becoming, Spartapuss," said Narkittus with a smile. "So our task is not to win a victory, but to prevent a tragedy. Clawdius needs his triumph. And worse, he would send the Mewids to Summerlands forever."

"Summerlands," I said. "That has a nice warm sound to it."

"It is the Mewid word for the Land of the Dead," said Narkittus, flicking his tail. "Or one of them," he added.

Perhaps he was having second thoughts about what he'd just said about me becoming very wise. For the truth is, for every moment of wisdom, I have ten moments of stupidity.

Narkittus leapt up onto a chair and declared: "Clawdius will not be happy until he is the father of ten thousand dead, and he stalks through Rome in triumph. Your old master must show his many enemies in the Senate that he is made of iron, when you and I know in fact he is made of, softer stuff. He looks to the blood of the Mewids to buy peace in Rome."

I thought that Narkittus had finished this speach when he suddenly asked. "And what does Spartapuss think? Is it a price worth paying?"

I thought for a moment and then replied, "I should not like to see any blood spilt, in this dark land or back in Rome."

Narkittus smiled. "It is in our power to prevent it. But we have only six weeks to stop a massacre."

"I will do whatever I can," I replied "on one condition… "

Narkittus stared at me for a long time and his tail began to flick. I don't suppose he had expected any conditions.

"And what might that condition be?" asked Narkittus, with a flick of the tail.

"Furg," I said. "You've got to get her out of there."

"That might prove difficult," said Narkittus.

"Tell them you need her for questioning, anything! There must be something you can do," I pleaded.

"She is unreliable," said Narkittus.

"She is young and hot-headed, but she's very brave," I said.

"Brave hearts and hot heads are not in short supply amongst the Kitons. They haven't done them much good so far. And they will not save the Mewids. She might endanger everything."

And without waiting for my reply, Narkittus stalked out into the night.

AUGUST XVIII

August 18th

Clawdius Arrives

TODAY THE EMPEROR Clawdius arrived. It was not a happy greeting, as his servants and freedcats strolled into the camp as if they owned the place and took over all of the good tents, including the one that Narkittus and I have made our home these past weeks. Clawdius's greeting to us was not warm, but at least he has found a use for me. He has employed me as a scribe for a travel book he is planning – Ten Weeks with the Barbarians. I fear that there is very little material to work with so far. He travelled down the Tiber to Ostia, along the coast and then through

Maul, partly by river and then by land before arriving at the Channel port. Apart from a couple of storms and an elephant that caught a mild cold, very little happened. Still, I have no doubt that the book will sell well at parties.

AUGUST XX

August 20th

CLAWDIUS'S ARRIVAL has not gone unnoticed. He has been here just one day and already we have reports that the enemy are on the move. Tomorrow General Mawlus holds a council of war. I am invited to attend, in my role as Clawdius's scribe. Narkittus will also attend. He has been silent since Clawdius arrived.

"What is wrong?" I asked. "Are you in danger, now that the Emperor is here?"

Narkittus laughed and replied, "It is far more dangerous to be away from his side." For Narkittus has rivals amongst Clawdius" other freedcats. And I am sure they have been whispering against him. He had risked much to come to this land and leave Clawdius back in Rome.

AUGUST XXI

21st August

TODAY I REPORTED to Clawdius's tent only to find Narkittus, General Mawlus and Vespurrsian and all of their attendants waiting outside. Frozen rain was coming down in pebbles and we were all glum by the time Clawdius let us in. He'd been 'having his breakfast' and he cannot stand being watched when he is eating. Now he was dozing on an enormous cushioned throne that had been hauled all the way from Rome, and looked rather out of place in a tent.

"We are at your service Emperor," said Narkittus in a soft voice, as if he was scared to wake the sleeping wolf.

"Service?" grunted Clawdius, half awake.

"Your officers have come to report to their Emperor," said Narkittus smoothly.

"Go on," said Clawdius, hauling himself up from his cushion. His eyes were watery and he had put on a lot of weight since I saw him last.

"This is the situation Emperor. Only the rebel Kiton Prince Caractapuss, stands between Rome and a glorious victory," said General Mawlus.

Clawdius cast a watery eye upon the General. Mawlus returned his stare. Something had got the Emperor twitching nervously. The fear of speaking in public perhaps? Or maybe he felt that other eyes were upon him? Clawdius had read many military books, with accounts of great battles and the tactics of famous Generals from the past. But the books didn't tell him what he needed to know. How much does an elephant eat every day? How do you get an army through a marsh? Too many questions had worked Clawdius up into such a state that he was unable to make decisions.

"We await your orders Emperor," said Mawlus.

Slowly, Clawdius grew still.

"These are my orders. We must s-s-s-send out our s-s-spies. Find this b-b-barbarian. Bring me his head on a plate," he spluttered.

"His location is not exactly a secret, Caesar," said General Mawlus.

Vespurrsian padded over to the back of the tent, undid the flaps and revealed an unlikely scene. The rain had died down, but it had not stopped. Strong sunlight fought its way past swollen clouds. From where the tent was pitched we had a great view of the hill opposite. It was rounded at the top with a sheer side. Here we saw something amazing. An enormous picture, in white lines, had appeared on the side of the hill. It was the image of a crowned cat with a long spear through his throat. Underneath, written in Catin letters, so big that they could be read ten miles away, was the words: DIE CLAWDIUS.

When the Emperor saw this terrible work of art, he fell onto the ground and began to cough, struggling to breathe. All in the tent stood in their places

– frightened to approach for fear that they might catch whatever the Emperor had. Only Narkittus kept his wits, ordering us all to leave the tent and calling for the doctors. I dared to move the Emperor and make him more comfortable. Ten minutes later he was able to get his first words out. It was something about Mewids and a curse. But there was no magic at work. We later learned that the great picture had been carved out of the white chalk of the hill.

Later that afternoon, Clawdius called Mawlus and Vespurrsian back and was able to continue. His mood was bad.

"Why haven't you ordered an attack?" he growled.

"I was obeying your last order, which was to await your orders, Emperor," said General Mawlus. "And if it wasn't for this Squeak meddler, I would have crushed the rebel and taken Camulod myself."

"Mark his words Emperor, 'I would have taken Camulod'," said Narkittus, slowly shaking his head. "What would the Inspector have to say about that?"

Clawdius looked horrified.

"For Rome, I mean. I would have taken the capital for my Emperor and Rome," growled General Mawlus.

"You will go after the rebel Prince," said Clawdius. "I will take C-c-camulod myself."

"An excellent plan. A triumph is as good as yours, Caesar," said Narkittus.

Mawlus nodded, realising that Narkittus had won the war of words.

"Leave me," said Clawdius.

General Mawlus padded slowly out of the tent. Then against his better judgement, he turned and asked: "But Emperor, what if the rebel prince runs?"

"Then you'd better be a faster runner General," said Narkittus, "if you ever want to run for the Senate, rather than running after rabbits at the circus."

Such was the confidence of Narkittus that he dared to speak to a General like that.

By nightfall tents had been struck, kit packed, blades sharpened and the camp was emptying. General Mawlus had already taken his legions, amounting to two thirds of the army's strength, to march west in pursuit of Caractapuss. His front ranks were ordered to march at the double in order to stop bunching in the lines, for the paths were narrow. The rest of us marched on Camulod, led by our Emperor and Vespurrsian. The Kiton's capital was fifty miles away – just two days' march at the double. We had not got far before we started to see bad signs. A great flock of crows headed in our direction. There were rumours passing up and down our lines saying that the crows were part of some bad magic that the Arch-Mewid had planned for us. On the first night we made camp in the rain at a miserable three-hut settlement. A sign in the local tongue said:

There was nothing to the place, not even a scratching post, so we made camp by an ancient stone that marked the crossing point of the river, where the water was shallowest. Although it was summer the river was swollen by the constant rain. It was too deep to cross without boats. Then, more whispers. This was a trick by Carac. He had doubled back on us. His warriors were waiting to ambush us, somewhere across the river.

Grassus sent word that Narkittus had summoned me to the Emperor's tent. Clawdius, puffed up at having put General Mawlus in his place, was now hungry for his triumph. As I entered, the Emperor was interrogating Vespurrsian. As ever, Narkittus was closer to the Emperor than his own shadow.

"Are you sure there will be enough?" asked Clawdius. Vespurrsian gave him a puzzled look. He didn't understand this question, so he ignored it and continued giving details from the spies' report.

"They're camped just out of sight, in a dip on the other side of the river, Caesar. It's a sizable force alright."

"There will be more than enough Caesar," said Narkittus with a smile.

"Tell the Inspector we will s-start the slaughter at dawn," said Clawdius, letting out a satisfied sigh.

Then he called for his doctors, who were ready with a bowl of steaming herbs, selected to bring good luck in battle, and gift him sleep.

"Where is your bridge Vespurrsian?" asked Narkittus. "It must be ready by first light."

Vespurrsian had arranged for a floating bridge to be built for the purpose of an easy crossing. But there had been problems getting it into position.

"It's on its way upriver, but it'll be here tonight," replied Vespurrsian.

"It had better be," said Narkittus. "General Mawlus has robbed us of all the best swimmers. And besides, the Emperor himself cannot swim."

Only Narkittus hung back as the Emperor's doctors waved us out of the tent. Making sure that Vespurrsian was in earshot, I turned to Grassus. "Who is this Inspector?" I asked. The old servant smiled.

"He's from the new military academy. The Senate have sent him to make sure that a triumph can be awarded."

"Can they do that?" asked Vespurrsian earnestly.

"Much has changed in Rome whilst we've been over here sir," growled Grassus.

"Spell it out for me," said Vespurrsian. "What exactly do these inspectors do?"

"They don't do anything sir," answered Grassus in a whisper. "They count."

"Count?" asked Vespurrsian in a puzzled voice. At that exact moment, Narkittus stalked past and our conversation ended as his servant hopped after him.

BRING ME WOMPS!

As I returned to my tent, the scent of Clawdius's herbs carried on the night air. But none of our dreams that night were sweet. As the stars rose, the wind got up. Those of us who poked our noses outside our tents could taste the enemy on the wind. By midnight the forest was lit by lightning strikes. Deep in the woods we heard the crack of falling trees. Legions of leaves blew across the river, and from the other side of the water there came a terrible howling. This bad night proved too much for some of Vespurrsian's lads. Many of them slunk off to bury their gold and valuables before the battle.

Clawdius had also had a bad night. His eyes were pale and watery. He dragged his bad leg behind him as he made his way to the riverbank to a spot out of range of the enemies' arrows, where the officers were waiting.

"The troops are er, really looking forward to your speech Caesar," said Vespurrsian, groping for words to fill the silence.

Clawdius gave him a dark look. He did not answer, instead he turned to Narkittus and began to splutter and choke. "The b-box?" he finally asked. "W-where are my W-W-Womps?"

"I have them here Caesar," said Narkittus. "But I don't think we'll have any need of magic. Your troops are ready. And however bad last night was for us, it was worse for the Kitons. Our spies tell us that they have very few tents."

"B-bring the box," ordered Clawdius.

Six attendants brought out the heavy wooden crate, slipping as they dragged it down the muddy bank. The crate was covered by a dirty grey cloth. The bearers slipped in the mud as they hauled it forward.

Vespurrsian lent very close to Narkittus and hissed.

"I thought you said that box went down with your first ship,' he growled.

Before Narkittus could answer, Clawdius sprung forward to meet the box, tearing off the cover to reveal the crate.

"Beware Caesar!" warned Narkittus. "It could be dangerous."

"It b-better be," laughed Clawdius.

We heard another terrible howl – like the ones that had kept us up all night. Then a crow landed on the bare oak on the other side of the river and let out a single caw.

"Ha!" said Clawdius, taking this for a good sign. He sprung at the box and began to struggle with the lid.

"Wait!" cried one of the bearers. "Do not open it Caesar. It may be cursed."

"You have had that box a while now, Narkittus.

What do you know about its secrets?" asked Vespurrsian.

"Well?" said Clawdius, turning to Narkittus.

Narkittus opened the lid of the crate just enough to reach inside, and from it he brought out a small yellow object and placed it carefully on the ground. I gave a gasp as I saw that it was a statue of a crouching cat, made entirely out of straw. It was a tiny version of the great wicker statue where I had been imprisoned.

"We believe that this ancient piece was made by the Arch-Mewid himself," said Narkittus.

"How does it work?" gasped Clawdius, in a state of extreme excitement.

"The whiskers come out, like this," said Narkittus, picking up the statue and pulling out one of the cat's straw whiskers. The tip of the 'whisker' was filed as sharp as a tooth.

"The straws are all of different lengths," Narkittus went on. "Our experts think that it must be some kind of ritual object," he said, offering the statue to Vespurrsian, who pulled out a long straw.

"Ritual?" said Clawdius. "Isn't that what the experts say when they haven't got a c-c-clue?" Then he drew a straw whisker from the statue. It was shorter than all the others. He threw it to the ground and hissed.

"Very little is known about the Mewid religion, Caesar," said Narkittus. "I fear it is beyond our knowledge."

"We n-need weapons!" hissed the Emperor. "Weapons of m-m-m-magical power!"

For what seemed like an age we waited while he stalked up and down the riverbank. He was furious and incapable of speech. But something held him back from looking inside the box himself. Finally it was Vespurrsian who spoke up.

"We've captured a prisoner Caesar," he said. "A Mewid who could reveal the secrets of the box."

"Where is this prisoner?" demanded Clawdius.

"In prison," said Vespurrsian.

"This is not wise Caesar. Mewid prisoners are most unreliable," said Nartkittus.

"Bring the prisoner to the b-b-bridge," ordered Clawdius.

"That may be a problem Emperor," said Vespurrsian.

"A problem?" asked Narkittus with a half smile.

"The bridge is on its way sir. They're paddling it down river as fast as they can. One of the elephants refused to get in the water," said Vespurrsian, looking at his notes. "Afraid of catching another cold it says," he added.

"B-b-bring me the Mewid," demanded Clawdius.

As we waited in silence, a breathless messenger arrived to say that the Inspector was here and wanted to meet us. Narkittus scribbled a note and handed it to the messenger, who tore off down the riverbank to deliver it.

The Mewid's Bargain

It wasn't long before soldiers arrived, wheeling a wooden cage. From it they brought out a bedraggled creature in torn robes. The jailer pushed the unfortunate beast onto the ground before Vespurrsian.

"Where's yer magic now?" laughed the guard. "That was just a taster," he jeered, thrusting the whip towards the prisoner's face. "Now answer the general's questions."

The Mewid got up without a fuss, ignored Vespurrsian and padded straight towards Clawdius.

"What can I do for you King Roman?" asked the prisoner.

Clawdius appeared pleased. "I will make a bargain with you Mewid," he said, without faltering.

"And what do you want in return Emperor. My tribe? My gods? The cream of my land? You have all of these things already."

"Do what I ask and I will g-gift you your life," said Clawdius.

"What about the pride of my ancestors?" asked the Mewid. "Answer me that."

Clawdius made no answer. He looked up at the clouds as if, by staring hard enough, he'd tell at what hour it would begin to rain again.

"I have a better bargain for you King Roman," said the Mewid. I'll do whatever you ask if you'll grant me the choice of one thing from the box to keep for myself."

"Impossible! You are in no position to bargain Mewid," warned Vespurrsian. The brindled guard reached for his whip again.

"I accept your bargain," said Clawdius. "Now show me."

There were howls as the Mewid approached the box. These gave way to gasps as its mysterious contents were tipped out upon the ground before us. All eyes were on Clawdius, but before he could speak a messenger burst through the crowd and fell on the ground in front of him.

"Message from the Inspector," gasped the messenger. "He wants to know why we haven't started yet and he wants to know where you are going to cross the river, so he can get a good view for the count."

Clawdius tore his gaze from the contents of the box and turned on Vespurrsian.

"Where is your b-bridge?" he hissed.

"It is coming Emperor!" cried Vespurrsian, shouting at the messenger to locate the bridge and tell the rowers to pull as if their lives depended on it (which indeed they did). Narkittus looked pleased to see the young commander squirm.

"Shall I tell the Inspector that there has been a change of plan Emperor?" he said sadly.

"And have the Senate make a m-m-mockery of me?" spat Clawdius, shaking with rage.

"How ignorant of me," said Narkittus, no longer looking so pleased with himself. "Please accept my most humble apologies Caesar."

Meanwhile, the hooded Mewid was carefully arranging the contents of the crate on the grey cloth. We all stared in wonder. And what was in the box? No golden crowns or silver relics. No jewel encrusted shields. The contents were: a rusted sword with half a blade, a mouldy wooden bowl with an eye carved into it, countless strange smelling balls of different sizes and a battered object covered in mud.

"Have you chosen?" asked Clawdius.

"I have chosen this," said the Mewid.

All eyes were on him as he picked up the muddy object. As the Mewid held it up for all to see, I realised that it was a battered old book. The Mewid flashed a knowing look in my direction. Suddenly, I recognised the face behind the hood. It was Furg.

"What in Paws name can the Mewid want with that?" whispered Clawdius, who had an interest in books.

For once Narkittus seemed so surprised that he seemed to have lost the power of speech.

At last he replied, "It is an ancient text by the look of it, Emperor."

Then I realised why the book looked familiar. It was my diary! I thought it had been lost in the marshes but somehow it had made its way into Narkittus's crate.

Furg gave me another knowing look. Why had she chosen my diary? It contained all of my secret thoughts and an account of my stay with the Mewids.

"What is it?" asked Clawdius.

Surely she did not plan to betray me?

"This," she said looking past the Emperor towards me, is a terrible book."

"No more games Mewid," hissed Vespurrsian. "Answer the Emperor."

My eyes met Furg's. Surely she would not betray me.

"It is the Sacred Book of Esnes Non," she said, "and now it is mine King Roman."

"Wouldn't you rather have this?" asked Clawdius, pawing at the broken sword.

"The Sword of Purlin?" said the Mewid in mock excitement. "No thanks."

"Why not?" asked Vespursian.

"It's blunt. We like our swords sharp in this land," laughed the Mewid, looking away over the water towards where the Kiton army was assembled, no doubt. This remark was not lost on Vespurrsian. He hissed in disapproval, baring his teeth.

The Mewid smiled back at him, pulled a whisker from the Straw Cat and began picking her teeth with it.

"There's your ritual Narkittus. It's a toothpick holder!" laughed Vespurrsian.

"What about this bowl with the Evil Eye on it?" asked Narkittus, ignoring him.

"That's one for the tourists," explained the Mewid. "That's not the Evil Eye, it's the Londump Eye."

"What are all these?" asked Narkittus, delicately holding up one of the wax balls.

"The Balls of Woool," announced the Mewid. "You'll be needing them later."

"Is that Woool – the ancient God of String?" asked Narkittus.

"Enough chatter old one," cried the Mewid. "I have chosen. The book is mine, a bargain is a bargain."

"T-take it!" spluttered Clawdius.

"Very well, Mewid. You have had your fun. Now you will show us how to use the magic balls," hissed Narkittus. "And they'd better be magic or it will go very badly for you."

I had never heard the diplomat speak like this before. He finished the sentence in a low growl, full of menace.

"Watch," commanded the Mewid. And she picked up one of the smallest balls and began to mutter under her breath. Her eyes glazed over, as if she was entering a trance. Then she leapt up and sprung towards the riverbank. The guards, caught by surprise for a moment, raised their weapons and rushed forward to block her path.

"Leave her!" commanded Narkittus.

At the very edge of the water the Mewid threw the ball towards the other bank. It rose in a high arc and landed with a crash that shook the very teeth in our mouths. A line of trees on the opposite bank burst into flames. Then, through the smoke, the front ranks of a large Kiton army were revealed.

Clawdius recoiled in a panic, cursing the Kitons, but he was clearly impressed by the Mewid's magic.

"We have no need of magic, Emperor," said Vespurrsian. "We have faced great hordes before and beaten them all."

Clawdius pawed at one of the largest balls and watched it roll.

"How do I work the spell?" he asked.

The Mewid drew closer to the Emperor and began to whisper some words in his ear. Clawdius soon began to repeat the Mewid's rhyme under his breath. Suddenly he sprung up and ran to the riverbank. The guards stared in disbelief at their Emperor as he threw the ball towards the far bank. But Clawdius was no great thrower. In his youth he had been too sick to take part in sports with the others. More recently, long years of laziness had wasted his muscles away. The ball fell with a plop into the river – mid-channel. The most dramatic effect was the disturbance of a family of ducks who had just surfaced after rooting for weeds. The mother duck spun around and gave the Emperor an accusing quack for frightening her babies.

The sight of this was too much for the assembled troops. Even the fear of death could not prevent them from howling with laughter.

"Mewid!" hissed Vespurrsian. "Why didn't you warn the Emperor that would happen?"

"I thought he could throw further than that," said

the Mewid, with a straight face. "He'll have to get in closer, the spell won't work unless the balls fall on land."

"What are you waiting for! Get me closer!" hissed Clawdius, gesturing at the guards to drag one of their boats into the water.

"Wait," growled Vespurrsian, as he took the sacred book of Esnes Non from the Mewid's grasp and gave it to me.

"Just so we're sure that there will be no more tricks!" said Vespurrsian. "If he tries anything, burn it," he added.

OUR INSPECTOR CALLS

Once again I was in possession of my diary. But I had no time to wonder at this, for at that very moment I became aware of a thin black cat who had appeared amongst us completely unnoticed. She took a long scroll out of a black case and began to make notes.

> *Time: plus one hour*
> *Location: Londump*
> *Enemy kills: nil*
> *Enemy prisoners: nil*
> *Enemy wounded: nil*

"Hold on – we haven't started yet!" said Vespurrsian.

"I'm afraid you have," said the Inspector. "One

hour before dawn, I have it right here in my notes."

"That's outrageous!" said Vespurrsian.

"Let me give you some free advice. Never argue. The Inspector's decision is final," said the Inspector.

Narkittus and Vespurrsian nodded.

"That's better," said the Inspector. She had a whining voice, like someone scratching their claws across fresh mosaic. "Triumphs do not grow on trees, you know." Then she turned to Vespurrsian and asked "Are you the commanding officer here?"

"He's not the c-c-commanding..." began Clawdius.

"Vespurrsian is not the commanding officer. It's is your Emperor who is in command," said Narkittus, pointing out Clawdius with a flourish. "I am Narkittus – his humble adviser."

The Inspector gave out a little grunt. "Well adviser, you should be humble. I don't like what I see. I like things to be done by the book. It's not my place to offer advice, but wouldn't some way of crossing the river be useful? If you want to attack the enemy before sundown, that is."

Before Narkittus could answer, the Inspector added "And you might like to remind the Emperor that to win a triumph he needs to be leading the attack. There are no triumphs unless he's in front of his army. That's the rules."

This was too much for Clawdius. He gathered up the remainder of the balls in a blanket and sprung towards the boat.

"Follow me!" he cried, leaping into the boat and motioning frantically for his bodyguards. There was just enough time for Narkittus and the Mewid to join him in the boat before the guards pushed off.

Vespurrsian, myself and the entire legion watched spellbound as they rowed the Emperor out into the middle of the channel. Although the sun was now higher in the sky, it was weak. Mist hung over the water. The river was swollen and the currents swirled this way and that.

No one, not even the Moracle herself, could have foreseen what was about to happen next. For just as the Emperor's boat was past the worst of the broken water, there came a shout from upriver. Vespurrsian's bridge had finally arrived. It was a narrow bridge in three sections, made of oak, and long enough to span the crossing point. But it seemed to have a mind of its own and somehow, whilst crossing some rapids upstream, it had broken free of its escort of soldiers and elephants. They were shouting warnings and they tore down the riverbank – trying to keep up with the runaway bridge. Pushed on by the flood of water, the first section of the bridge came rushing down the middle of the channel.

The Emperor's bodyguards heard these cries and seeing the danger, managed to get the prow of their boat out of the way, pushing the offending bridge off with their spears. They were just breathing sighs of relief when the second section of the bridge hit the Emperor's boat square on the stern and knocked the occupants into the churning water. Whether by chance or careful planning, the Kitons chose this moment to begin their attack. A volley of arrows fell just short of our side of the bank. I was taking all of this in when I heard Narkittus shouting. He'd made his way to the edge of the upturned boat.

"The Emperor! The Emperor! He cannot swim!"

The heroic thing to do at this point would have been to jump into the raging water, with no thought for my own safety, in order to swim to the aid of Clawdius. As a burning arrow hissed into the water in front of me, it occurred to me that I have never been a particularly strong swimmer. If the flaming arrows, which the Kitons seemed to have in good supply, did not get me, there was a fair chance that I would die of cold if I dived in. I wondered what might lurk beneath the churning waters. Freshwater crocodiles or pond spiders or the white headed Kitish leech? I have a horror of leeches for I cannot bear the sight of my own blood.

"Will nobody save the Emperor?" said the Inspector, shaking her head and reaching for her notes.

"The Emperor! The Emperor!" cried Vespurrsian.

As the chaos had unfolded, he had crouched stone still on the riverbank. He now turned on his soldiers, shouting at them to stop staring and act - swim to the Emperor's aid, if they valued their eyes.

Three figures had by now managed to climb on top of Clawdius's stricken craft. One was Furg, her Mewid's gown now soaked and as heavy as armour, while two auxiliaries were attempting to haul Clawdius out to safety. They'd almost got him out of the water when there was a cry. Furg began to topple and lost her footing. She waved for a moment, like a larch in a gale, and at last she fell face down into the water. This set the boat rocking and the two guards tumbled out into the river like dirty water from a bucket.

Then a familiar voice beside me said "Spartapuss, listen carefully, for there is little time. You must save the Emperor. Get him to the other bank or all will be lost."

In disbelief I spun around. The voice I'd heard belonged to my old mentor, the mystic who had trained me in the martial arts. But there was only the Inspector there beside me.

I stared open-mouthed for a moment, "Tefnut?" I whispered, "I feared that you were dead!"

"Not so," replied the Inspector as I caught sight of her big eyes flashing from behind her disguise. "At least, not yet by Sun and Moon. There is no time for reunions. Help the Emperor. I will save your Mewid friend if she can be saved."

"Furg!" I cried in a panic. I had been so unsettled by Tefnut's appearance that I had forgotten her. I scanned the water for the spot where I had seen her last.

"Go now! Before she is beyond my help!" ordered Tefnut.

I stared at the spot where the Mewid had been knocked off the boat. There was no sign of her, only muddy water. Everything that Tefnut had just said emptied from my mind.

"Furg! I'm coming! I'm coming!" I shouted. I took three steps back and plunged into the raging flood. Immediately I felt a claw at my collar, dragging me back to the bank. Tefnut gave me a withering look.

"Fool!" she said. "I will help your friend. You must save the Emperor!" And she pressed a round object into my outstretched paw. "Keep him on that side of the river, for he has a triumph to win. If you are in danger, say the watchword: "Sword of Purlin". I will save your friend."

I nodded in agreement, although my list of questions could have filled a medium-sized scroll.

"And use the boat!" said Tefnut pointing at the riverbank, her tail flicking in agitation. "Go! Do you think I'm made of magic?"

I saw that a second boat had been made ready. Jumping in, I grabbed the oars and began to row towards the opposite bank. A thick curtain of mist was rising and wrapping itself around the boat. Somehow I knew that no arrows could fall inside this white curtain. By rights I should have been rushed downstream by the current. But this boat seemed to have a mind of its own and it was working its way back upstream. Puzzled, I looked over the side of the boat, only to witness a sight beyond understanding. The river was flowing backwards. There was a smell on the mist, like dried mistletoe burning.

I looked around me, trying to get a sight of Clawdius but my hope soon sank. The muddy water was full of debris - wooden planks from the bridge, arrows and spears, all churning around like dirty washing. Once again I had followed Tefnut's orders without question. I had failed her before at the quayside back in Rome and now I was about to fail her again. How in Peus's name was I supposed to find Clawdius in all of this? Mystics are mysterious by nature, but why she bothered with me I had no clue.

Just then something heavy hit the boat. It was a section of the bridge, now floating upstream by means of something other than the current. Clinging to it, like a reluctant water rat, was the Emperor of the Known World.

The hardest part was getting him to pull his claws in and let go. When we were both safely aboard I pushed away at the section of bridge to try to free the boat. The current did the rest and, after some effort on my part, we managed to make it to the bank.

Looking back across the river I saw that the Romans on the opposite bank were running after the sections of Vespurrsian's bridge like a pack of blind dogs after a rabbit. They were nowhere near crossing the river and engaging the enemy. I learned later that General Mawlus had taken all the Batavians with him, leaving the Emperor without any trained swimmers. Clawdius and I were the only Romans who had made it into Kiton territory.

"Are you hurt, Emperor?" I asked.

Clawdius shook his head, speechless with shock. I mouthed my silent thanks to Fortune for bringing us to the safety of dry land. Then I realised that 'safety' was not the right word for where we now found ourselves. The Kitons, encouraged by their early success with the flaming arrows, had come out of the wood and formed their chariots up into a great line. They might start the charge at any moment. I wondered if anyone had told the Kiton chiefs that I, Spartapuss, was trying to help their cause and save the Mewids from destruction. It was possible, but Kiton chiefs are not Generally good on details when they are in the middle of a chariot charge.

"Stay down," I said, begging Clawdius to take cover.

A single chariot had come out of the line and was now heading towards the river. The driver shouted a command and a crow flew up from his side and gave out three loud caws.

"Why just one chariot?" asked Clawdius. "Why d-d-don't they all just c-c-charge?"

"I think they may be scouting our position. Or perhaps they're going to offer us a truce?" I said hopefully.

"Die Clawdius! Death to the Idiot King!" shouted the driver of the chariot.

Clawdius looked at me with a mixture of horror and annoyance.

"Don't worry, that's just a battle cry. I don't think we've been spotted," I whispered. The crow wheeled high in the air and spoke again in his cracked voice. The chariot changed direction. Now it was heading straight towards us.

Then I heard another shout. "Death to the Gingers! Death to the Turntails!

"Are they still ab-b-b-bout to offer us a truce?" asked Clawdius.

I searched for cover but there was none. We were alone on a muddy hill, dotted with rabbit holes. The stump of a fallen tree, rotted by the rain, was the only place worth running to. I looked back towards the river. Surely now we would be safer afloat than facing the entire Kiton army alone on the plain?

"At least we have not burnt our boats," I said. "Didn't one of the philosophers say that retreat is nobler than defeat?"

Clawdius nodded.

As these words left my lips, a flaming arrow flew over our head and shivered into the middle of our boat. There must have been some magic at work for the wet timbers lit up like a candle and began to blaze with a weird green flame.

Here we stood, beyond all help – only the Gods

could save us now. In tales of old this is the point where the heroes draw their swords and take their own lives rather than let themselves get taken by the enemy. But I had no sword. Then I saw Clawdius scrambling towards the largest rabbit hole.

"D-d-dig! Dig!" he spluttered.

I joined him at the mouth of the hole. The earth was soft and easy to dig and the Emperor had already set to the task of making it wider.

"This is madness," I began, the Kitons have dogs. They are sure to get a scent of us."

"Be silent and d-dig," said Clawdius.

Soon the mouth of the rabbit hole was opened up so that it was wide enough to squeeze inside and, as we dug down, side tunnels began to collapse into the main hole. The Emperor squeezed backwards and disappeared down the hole. I poked my head in after him and was about to follow when something bit me hard on the nose. I howled in pain.

"Get out!" hissed Clawdius. "F-f-find your own hole!"

"There is no time, the Kitons are upon us," I said. "And if they find me, they'll surely find you too."

The Emperor of the Known World snarled. "You will d-d-defend my life," he hissed.

Then I remembered the object that Tefnut had given me. The ball was soft and waxy to the touch. It was a pale white colour and a little bigger than the one the Mewid had thrown before.

"Do you know what this is?" I asked.

The Emperor nodded.

"When the time comes, use it," I said, passing it carefully into his claws.

It wasn't long before we heard the baying of hounds and a scrambling of paws. The Kitons were above us, so close that we could hear their voices. Not wanting to wait for the snapping of jaws, I decided to face them. I squeezed my way up through the roof of a side tunnel and clawed my way out. As I stood blinking in the light, I found myself nose to nose with a huge Kiton chieftain, armed with a broadsword.

Watchwords! I have never been any good at remembering them. I have tried everything: repeating them to myself over and over again, making a picture in my mind, making up a song out of them, but still I find that when I need to remember them, my mind goes blank. True to form, I hunted the halls of my mind for the watchword that Tefnut had given me but didn t get a sniff of it.

The Kiton warrior ran a long claw down the blade of his sword and began to mutter softly. I have always thought there is something strange about giving a sword a 'pet' name and whispering prayers over it before battle. The Purrmanians are known for this sort of thing but the Kitons are absolutely the worst when it comes to such superstitions.

Suddenly a thought entered my head. "The watchword is 'Sword' I declared in triumph."

"Sword of what?" demanded the Kiton. He was a warrior of the Sillures tribe, and they were not known for their patience. He ran his claw down the blade of his sword once again and his thick tail began to beat the ground.

"Sword of Paws!" I declared, knowing that was not the right answer.

"Wrong!" said the warrior, shaking his head.

"For Peus's sake!" I exclaimed.

"Wrong again!" cried the Kiton, taking this for an answer.

"That wasn't a guess," I protested. "You've already told me that the answer has "Sword" in it."

"Last chance," hissed the warrior.

"Sword of Peus?" I offered, though I knew in my heart that this was wrong as well.

"Enough!" growled my enemy. The whiskers on my right side gave a twinge. He took two steps forward and aimed his sword towards my head in a thrust that would have kebabbed me if I'd stood still. Luckily, I'd anticipated the blow and rolled to my left. The broadsword made a high whooshing noise as it swished through the air.

"Stop!" I cried. "Wait!... don't kill me!"

"Why not?" asked the warrior wearily. He was not used to so much chatter during battle.

"At least tell me the correct answer before I die," I begged.

"Purlin!" said the Kiton. "It was Sword of Purlin."

"I was so close!" I moaned.

"Close," said the Kiton, raising the sword again.

"N-n-n-n-naarrrgh!" groaned a voice below me.

For the Kiton, it must have been a sight to behold. An earth clad figure pushing its way out of the red soil, like some long dead ancestor from Summerlands, back from the grave for a visit.

"N-n-n-aarrgh!" groaned Clawdius again.

"Great Mother!" cried the Kiton. His eyes fell upon the figure of the Emperor of the Known World, who was covered from head to tail in red mud.

"Come!" I cried, grabbing Clawdius by the collar. The chariot was our only hope of escape. In a panic we both scrambled on.

"Ha!" I cried, tugging on the reins and trying to sound professional. I had read somewhere about 'The Voice of Command" which you were supposed to use with dogs. It was very simple really, all to do with confidence and being masterful. "Ha! Ha!" I cried again with whatever confidence I could muster.

The lead dog, who had been dozing, got slowly to her feet. She looked back at me and then turning her head to one side, she let out a yelp.

"Don't you dare!" growled the warrior, shaking his fist. The dog looked from me to her master and back again, then stood still. I knew who I'd obey, if I was on a leash.

Clawdius grabbed a whip from a hook in the

chariot and began to strike out. But the Kiton warrior caught the end of the whip and pulled it from his grasp, almost dragging the Emperor from the chariot.

With an enormous bang, a missile thrown from a Roman ballista struck the ground to the left of us. The dogs needed no more encouragement. They sprung to their feet in a panic and began to run. I wrestled with the reins but it was no use. "Halt! Halt!" I cried confidently, but it was no good, they were running wild. Our chariot wheeled in a wide circle and swung away from the river. In vain I heaved on the reins and tried to shout masterfully, but the dogs paid no mind to my shouts or Clawdius's curses.

Now we were heading straight for the line of shields where the mass of the Kiton army were waiting. We were so close now that we could see the emblems on their shields. I shall not go into details of the Kiton's shield paintings, for many of them were most offensive.

Clawdius smiled. "It is just as the Mewid foretold," he said. His eyes hardened as he held up the magic ball.

"Hear my p-prayer Esnes Non, Destroyer of Worlds," whispered Clawdius. "D-d-d-death come to them on swift wings. Send them to S-S-Summerlands."

And with that he cast the ball towards the Kitons shield wall. But his throw was weak. Although we were close, the white ball rolled up towards the Kiton lines and bounced tamely against a shield.

I remember little of what happened next. There was a great flash and a noise like a thousand oaks felled by lightning. Then there was smoke. A huge cloud of white smoke, which still hung in the air when I came to. As my eyes opened I saw a familiar face above me.

"Tef... " I began but a ladle full of cold water stopped my tongue.

"What say you Inspector?" asked Vespurrsian, in a state of great excitement.

I dragged myself up and took in the scene. I was in a makeshift tent with the Emperor, the Inspector, Narkittus and Vespurrsian. Our forces had finally got Vespurrsian's bridge together and were pouring across the river in single file.

The Inspector was staring across the hill, towards the spot where the Kiton army had stood. A few pockets of white mist hung in the air. Fires spat and smouldered in the heavy drizzle. A lone crow circled mournfully but he had no hope of a feast for the Kiton army was gone. Only their shields and spears remained – still in a wall, with spear tips up towards the sky. Then the rain began to fall.

"This is most irregular. I do not know what to say," declared the Inspector finally. "That was one of the largest enemy forces that I have ever seen. But where have they gone? There aren't any dead to count."

"Count this, Inspector," said Narkittus, pawing at

a pile of white dust.

"The Mewid's magic must have blown them from this world to the next."

"Straight to S-s-summerlands," declared the Emperor, with a gleam in his watery eye.

"Well Inspector? What say you? Is it a triumph for the Emperor?" asked Vespurrsian in excitement.

Just as the Inspector was about to speak, a messenger hurried in. He looked a sorry state, for he was soaked to the skin.

"It's from the kings of the Kitons, Emperor," said Narkittus. "It seems they are now ready to surrender and accept an alliance with Rome."

"What nonsense!" said Vespurrsian. "We've just defeated them in battle. We haven't even offered them the chance to surrender yet."

Narkittus sighed loudly.

"Emperor, this message comes from the tribes who did not take part in the battle. It seems they were waiting to see what would happen. This land needs a strong leader in order to stop the tribes from warring amongst themselves. Their message is addressed to Iron Clawdius.

"Iron C-c-clawdius you say?" said the Emperor, delighted. He had been given plenty of nicknames before, but none of them were the sort of name that you'd be happy to carve onto a column or an arch.

"Well Inspector, what do you say?" asked Vespurrsian again. His tail flicked against a pole. This opened a seam in the canvas, and a puddle that had collected in the roof poured down through the gap and began to soak the cushioned throne.

"I d-do n-not know about you Inspector, but I have been four d-d-days in this wretched land - and that is four d-d-days too long!" hissed Iron Clawdius, leaping from the throne and advancing towards the Inspector, claws out.

The Inspector backed away, head low to the ground and whispered "Very well Emperor, I think we have had sufficient."

AUGUST XXIV

August 24th

Unhappy Returns

S O IT WAS THAT Iron Clawdius met the eleven Kings of the Kitons at Camulod and they accepted his terms for surrender. They had no choice. All in the south of the land made peace with Rome and accepted Clawdius as their Emperor. Only Carac still made war on Rome, but he was lost in the wilds of the west, with General Mawlus on his tail.

Messages were sent to the Senate and arrangements for Clawdius's triumph were made. In addition, the Senate declared that Clawdius should have an arch built near Londump, with his statue placed on top, and the signs of the eleven kings carved underneath. This was to be started as soon as our masons could get decent stone in good quantities.

When the ceremonies were over, Clawdius got ready to go home. He had come through flood, fire and battle, but it may have been the proposal of marriage from Queen Catimandua of the Micini tribe that frightened him into a hasty return to Rome.

I was tucking into a bowl of wall fish when Narkittus came in unannounced and thrust a bundle into my hand.

"A present from your Fleagyptian friend," he said.

"My diary!" I cried, delighted to have got the book back in one piece. I thought that I'd lost it once again but it seemed to keep coming back to me.

"Any news of our friend the Inspector?" I asked.

"None," said Narkittus. "Gone to Rome, with the Emperor's party, I suppose."

Narkittus cast me a look as if he was waiting for me to confirm this information for him.

"Oh," I said, trying not to sound too disappointed whilst sucking the remains of a snail from its shell. I suppose I should have expected as much. Mystics are not good at goodbyes.

"I don't suppose you've found me anywhere better to sleep?" I asked.

I was now sleeping in a storage hut, the Emperor's followers having taken all of the good tents for themselves when they left for Camulod. My hut had been previously occupied by some chickens and a goat. The latter had left a strong reminder of himself all over the earth floor.

I set the diary down carefully and picked up where I'd left off with the bowl of snails.

"Keep it safer this time," said Narkittus. "It was brave of your young friend to prevent its discovery."

He was trying to warm himself, but the heat from the single log fire was too weak for serious warming.

"What news of Furg?" I asked. "It's been days since Tefnut rescued her. Surely she's well enough to see me now?"

"She is fully recovered, I am told. She's not too pleased with any of us right now. But she played her part brilliantly." Narkittus looked up from the fire. "What a performance as the Arch-Mewid!" he exclaimed. "The Sacred Book of ESNES NON indeed! Clawdius believed every word of it. Just as he believed that his magic ball blasted his enemies into dust! What marvellous NON SENSE."

"Did you know it was nonsense?" I asked, sensing that he had something else to tell me. "About the book I mean?"

"Naturally," laughed Narkittus. "How could the Mewids have a magic book? The Kitons cannot read or write."

"Not even the Mewids?" I asked.

"Especially not the Mewids," he replied, flicking a

stray twig back to the fire. "Didn't you learn anything at Mewid school? Their storytellers must remember everything without writing it down. They call it "learning by heart" and they are convinced that any type of writing is false learning. Why would they have a magic book?"

I gazed into the fire. As the flames finally got a proper hold and the green wood began to hiss, a question began to form in my mind.

"What about the letter? The one that started this war?" I asked. "Give us back our Weapons of Magical Power, or you will Die Clawdius." "If the Kitons have no writing, who wrote that?"

"Spartapuss," began Narkittus, "There are some plans that are too big for you or me to understand. Your Fleagyptian friend would tell you the same."

I stared at him in disbelief. "You mean that you planned this whole invasion?" I gasped. "What right have you to meddle in the affairs of another land?"

"Spoken like a true Kiton," said Narkittus. "Clawdius is the ruler of the known world. It was felt that he was a weak ruler. He needed this invasion to make him strong, and prevent a more terrible war between Roman and Roman. The Empire may seem solid and uncrackable but, in truth, all such works are never more than a few steps away from ruin."

The skin of the green log was blistering under the heat and it suddenly spat. The whiskers on my right side gave a sudden twinge.

"Good evening," said Narkittus, without turning towards the door. Once again he seemed to have an extra pair of eyes in the back of his head.

"Is it?" hissed Furg. "I can't see any good in it. Clawdius has taken my country. Our leaders have sold us down the river and even your friend's magic can't make it flow backwards."

Furg's eyes were wild and she would not hold my gaze. She looked smaller and leaner than I remembered.

"It's better than being butchered, I should think," said Narkittus.

"Really? I expect that's why the tribes in the north are rioting! They're all so happy to be under Roman rule."

"Clawdius has made the Kiton friendlies into client kings," said Narkittus wearily. "Do you know what that means? You won't even be ruled directly from Rome. Each tribe will look after its own, just like before."

Furg sprung towards him with a hiss.

"It was the best agreement you could hope for. The Senate was not happy with it I can assure you," said Narkittus, standing his ground.

"You have made slaves of us all," hissed Furg. I thought she was going to strike him.

"That might have been better," said Narkittus, "but the Senate decided that it would be easier to take your taxes instead. After all you've been paying taxes to Rome for years, haven't you?"

"Furg," I began, "I can see that you're upset... "

Narkittus's arguments had force. But his cool words only made her temper hotter. Now she was rocking back on her haunches, preparing to spring at him.

"Your tribe have sworn to keep the peace," warned Narkittus.

"My father! The peacemaker," she spat the words out like a bad oyster.

"What will you do now?" I asked, keen to fill the silence. "Back to Mewid School, I suppose?"

Furg let out a little half hiss. "What do you care? You're going back to Rome."

This was news to me. She could tell by my look that her barbed words had found their mark.

"Didn't he tell you? Your ship arrives tonight."

"Where did you hear that?" asked Narkittus, bristling.

"Right here, last night," answered Furg. "If I were you, I'd keep your voice down, unless the spies have fur in their ears."

I glared at Narkittus.

"Goodbye Romans. I hope you are packed for a triumph. Never return to this land. Your kind is not welcome here. You have been warned," said Furg.

Perhaps I should have taken more notice of this warning but I was still getting over the news of our departure.

"Well Narkittus, is it true? Are we leaving tonight?" I demanded.

"This is not the time or the place to discuss the matter," he answered gruffly.

"Not the time? When exactly were you planning to tell me?" I asked. "Why in the name of Peus am I always the last one to know about the important things?"

Furg was wrong about me but I could not find words to explain it. I had wanted to help the Kitons. Not all Romans are corrupt and rotten. I for one was not looking forward to returning for the Emperor's triumph.

"Furg," I began, turning towards her. But I was talking to thin air. She had slipped out into the night. In a panic, I followed her, calling her name aloud despite Narkittus's protests that it was no use. But my cries were lost in the wind and rain. When I returned some hours later, Narkittus was waiting where I had left him.

"Are you ready?" he asked.

Ready or not, I had to go. I had nothing to pack anyway, except for this diary. Silently, we crept off to the edge of the camp. Narkittus gave the guard the watchword and we slipped away without fuss.

About a mile out of camp we picked up a small track and began to wind our way down towards a line of trees that marked the line of the river. The rain had eased but the wind was getting up. Thin clouds blew quickly across the face of the moon. A few minutes later we had reached the bank. It was wide here, far too wide to swim, and there were no boats in sight. Although I had not seen one, I shivered at the thought of the long-snouted river crocodiles that are famous in this land. So I said a silent prayer to Terminus, the God of Cancellations, to watch over me.

Narkittus also looked nervous, he sat patiently on a rotten log and waited.

"Where will Furg go now?" I asked. Then thinking aloud I said, "Not back to school, by the sound of it."

"They would not have her back," said Narkittus. "Now she is one of the 'forgotten', for she has broken their laws. Now she must fend for herself."

"That is harsh," I said.

"Hard but fair," said Narkittus. "The Kitons believe it is an excellent system. For it keeps good order. Some would argue that we should try something similar in Rome instead of spoiling our young from the litter and breeding a city of little tyrants."

I took it from this that Narkittus had little time for the young.

"Everyone deserves a second chance,' I said. "Furg was only trying to help the Mewids. And what thanks does she get for it? Why do the Mewids have such cruel laws?"

"Ask them yourself," said Narkittus. From around the bend in the river came a long boat. I was filled with wonder at the sight of such a craft. It looked like an ancient design; a seagoing boat with a flat hull and oars as well as a sail. It was a marvel to see a sail so far inland. As the ship drew closer, I saw that it was crewed entirely by Mewids, with one exception.

"Ahoy shipmates!" cried a voice. "Prepare to come aboard."

I recognised the voice of Captain Kat.

"Ready!" called Narkittus.

"Speak for yourself," I cried. "I'm not getting on board their ship."

"She's not their ship, she's mine," cried Kat. "At least she is while I'm Captaining her." He sprung into a rowing boat and began to strike out towards us.

"I mean it," I said when Kat had brought the boat alongside the bank. "The last time I met your Mewid friends, they were making preparations to turn me into a sacrifice."

"Surely not?" laughed Kat. "They have been very worried about you. They've had spies out and everybody looking for you."

"Come closer," I whispered. "Listen Kat. They made me do a kind of a test to become a Mewid. They put me into this hideous statue of a cat that was all made of wicker."

"They told me," said Kat. "They said you took the test, and you were gone when the morning came. Now get in this boat before every spy in the land knows our business."

"Wait!" I cried. "That night in the wicker statue. I left because... "

"Come!" said Kat.

"Because they were going to set the statue on fire with me inside!"

"Nonsense," said Narkittus.

"I saw the smoke," I said. "With my own eyes."

"Smoke?" said a voice beside me on the bank. I became aware that a sudden mist had descended, and out of it padded a figure in white.

"Smoke," I said again, for I would not let this pass.

"You saw the smoke from our underground heating. I ordered them to fire it up, for I know you Romans are not used to the cold and damp of our Kitish nights."

"Peus be praised!" I said with relief. "I thought... "

"You thought that we were going to sacrifice you to our Gods," said the Arch-Mewid. "That Mewlius Caesar has a lot to answer for. He has the most vivid imagination, but he knows nothing of our ways."

Now I felt foolish. "Furg pointed out the smoke," I muttered in my defence.

"Furg said a lot of things. Some she thought were true and some she wanted to be true," said Narkittus.

"Will she return to her father then?" I asked.

"To her father? No."

"But she is fond of her aunt, I believe."

"Are you certain?" said Narkittus. "I think she has

gone to join Carac, in the wilds of the west. If so, she is lost. For he cannot win against General Mawlus."

"Come aboard all of you," said Kat.

Narkittus and the Arch-Mewid leapt into the boat.

"So now I must climb aboard and return to Rome and leave her? Is that it?" I asked.

"First we are bound for the Sacred Isle of Anglesey," said Narkittus.

"Right under the Roman's noses," said Kat. "Now come aboard before we are discovered."

I made ready to leap aboard but stopped and stood on the bank, staring out over the grey water. I wondered who was right. Carac and his fighters or the Mewids with their secrets? Could anyone really own a land, any more than the fish owned the river? The land of my birth was strange indeed, where some tribes welcomed outsiders with friendship, but others made war with each other over a favourite dog or a few chickens. Romans, auxiliaries, Kitons and Mewids, perhaps we were all strangers in this land. I heard a splash above me. A heron dived for a fish and caught it. I noticed that it had stopped raining.

"I'm not coming," I said, stepping backwards onto the bank.

"Spartapuss," said Kat.

"I must find her," I replied. The look that I gave Kat must have convinced him.

"As you wish," said Narkittus, shaking his head.

"Good luck then shipmate!" said Kat, pushing away from the bank.

"Farewell Spartapuss! Your name will be remembered in our tales and songs," said the Arch Mewid.

"Remember me in your tales please, never mind the songs," I replied, recalling the terrible wailing that passes for music in this land.

Slowly Kat brought the little boat alongside the ship.

"Wait!" I called. "Where will I find Furg's aunt?"

"Walk east," said the old Mewid, "to the lands of the Micini tribe."

"Thank you," I cried. "And what name shall I ask for?"

"Boudicat," came the reply. "Ask for Boudicat."

I AM SPARTAPUSS

By Robin Price

In the first adventure in the Spartapuss series...
Rome AD 36. The mighty Feline Empire rules the world.
Spartapuss, a ginger cat is comfortable managing Rome's
finest Bath and Spa. But Fortune has other plans for him.
Spartapuss is arrested and imprisoned by Catligula, the
Emperor's heir. Sent to a school for gladiators, he must
fight and win his freedom in the Arena - before his oppo-
nents make dog food out of him.

'This witty Roman romp is history with cattitude.'
Junior Magazine (Scholastic)

ISBN 10: 09546576-0-8
ISBN 13: 978-0-9546576-0-4

UK £6.99
USA $14.95/ CAN $16.95

For USA/ Canada orders contact:
Independent Publishers Group
Phone: 312.337.0747
FAX: 312.337.5985
http://www.ipgbook.com/

Download free Spartapuss wallpaper at
www.mogzilla.co.uk

CATLIGULA

By Robin Price

Was this the most unkindest kit of all?

In the second adventure in the Spartapuss series...

Catligula becomes Emperor and his madness brings Rome to within a whisker of disaster. When Spartapuss gets a job at the Imperial Palace, Catligula wants him as his new best friend. The Spraetorian Guard hatch a plot to destroy this power-crazed puss in an Arena ambush. Will Spartapuss go through with it, or will our six-clawed hero become history?

ISBN 09546576-1-6
978-0-9546576-1-1

UK £6.99
USA $10.95/ CAN $14.95

For USA/ Canada orders contact:
Independent Publishers Group
Phone: 312.337.0747
FAX: 312.337.5985
http://www.ipgbook.com/

Download free Spartapuss wallpaper at www.mogzilla.co.uk

COUNT MILKULA
A tale of milk and monsters

By Woodrow Phoenix & Robin Price

Lemmy's world is rocked when he loses his bedroom to his new baby brother. So he turns to Granny for comfort and a bedtime story. She tells the tale of Count Milkula, a selfish, noisy, milk-crazed creature from the monotonous mountains of Mamsylvania. Lemmy finds out that, like baby brothers, Mampires can't do anything for themselves. That's why looking after them is such an adventure.

For ages 5 and up
32 pages
Full colour illustrations

ISBN 0-9546576-5-9 • 978-0-9546576-5-9
Hardback: UK £11.99 USA $22.95 CAN $24.95

ISBN 0-9546576-6-7 • 978-0-9546576-6-6
Paperback: UK £5.99 USA $14.95 CAN $16.95

For USA / Canada orders contact:
Independent Publishers Group
Phone: 312.337.0747
FAX: 312.337.5985
http://www.ipgbook.com/

SANTA CLAUS IS ON A DIET

By Nancy Scott-Cameron & Craig Conlan

Mrs Claus looked Santa up and down
She shook her head, began to frown
'Santa dearest, the problem's that
in plain words darling,
you're too fat!'

With narrow chimneys now a danger, Mrs Claus decides that it's time for Santa to cut down on calories. The reindeer, keen to lighten their load, are only too happy to help. But there's a fatal flaw in their weight loss plan. Is Santa on a crash diet?

For ages 4 and up
32 pages • Full colour illustrations
Available: 01/09/07

ISBN 09546576-9-1 • 978-0-9546576-9-7
Paperback: UK £5.99 USA $14.95 CAN $16.95

For USA / Canada orders contact:
Independent Publishers Group
Phone: 312.337.0747
FAX: 312.337.5985
http://www.ipgbook.com/

ABOUT THE AUTHOR

Robin Price was born in Wantage in 1968. Before going to work in Japan, Robin left his cat, Bleep, with his mum and dad. When he returned, Bleep was as fat as a barrel. His parents had followed the instructions on the cat food: 'Feed your cat as much as it can eat. Cats regulate their own diet and seldom overeat'.

I Am Spartapuss is Robin's first novel. The sequel, *Catligula,* was published in 2005. His third novel, *Die Clawdius* was published in 2006.